Madame de Pompadour

The Making of a Mistress

By Nichole Christakes Dapelo

Author of European Women in History

PUBLICATION CONSULTANTS
We Believe In The Power Of Authors

PO Box 221974 Anchorage, Alaska 99522-1974
books@publicationconsultants.com — www.publicationconsultants.com

ISBN 978-1-59433-761-1
eBook ISBN: 978-1-59433-762-8
Library of Congress Catalog Card Number: 2017960729

Copyright 2017 Nichole Christakes Dapelo
—First Edition—

All rights reserved, including the right of
reproduction in any form, or by any mechanical
or electronic means including photocopying or
recording, or by any information storage or
retrieval system, in whole or in part in any
form, and in any case not without the
written permission of the author and publisher.

Manufactured in the United States of America.

To my husband, my best friend, my beloved

CHAPTER I

"It's impossible," declared the Mother Superior of the Ursuline Convent, her piercing blue eyes were nearly hidden under her hooded eyelids, yet still had the power to penetrate. "Your request is out of the question."

I stood there, holding my mother's hand and looking up at her face.

"It is not a request," Mother replied. Her voice was gentle and calm, but her face was resolute.

"At least wait until her father returns. You are subjecting this child to danger, you have no means, no resources to be responsible for a little girl on your own, you can hardly manage to take care of your own matters," the nun pleaded.

"The means have been secured." Her voice now grew firm. "I will have my child." And turning towards me, she picked me up in her arms and walked away.

I expected a rented carriage to be waiting for us, we could never afford such an expense before, but instead I found awaiting us one of the most lavish carriages I'd ever seen.

"Is this ours, Mama?"

She smiled and patted my hand. "It was a gift… from someone who loves you very much, to welcome you home."

The streets of Paris were at their most enchanting during the early morning hours, when the day was new and the cobblestone streets were fresh with dew. My mother's hand warmed my little fingers as we scurried past the *pâtisserie*.

"Mother, may we stop, just for a moment?" I said, pausing in front of the bakery.

"When we return, *ma petite*," she promised, rubbing my cold little hands between her own on this chilly winter morning. "I'm taking you to someplace very special today." Turning to me, she removed her emerald green glove and placed her cool palm on my forehead to feel my temperature. "Are you feeling well, darling?" And I nod my head 'yes,' though my throat did hurt. Even at that tender age, I had grown accustomed to enduring my poor health, but did my best to save my mother from worrying.

I had only just returned from the convent at Poissy. There, I was under the loving and dutiful eye of my father's sisters, the nuns at the Ursuline convent, where I spent the past three years while my father was away. He had left for Germany when I was four years old. I can still remember listening to the harshly whispering voices of my parent's arguing, my father trying to explain that he had no choice but to leave, some sort of scandal having to do with the corn supply in Paris and how fortune had betrayed him, claiming that he was being used as a scapegoat. He begged my mother to understand and to forgive him, stressing the injustice of it all. Surely this was not his fault; he had no choice but to go. My mother, notably the most beautiful woman in Paris, could land on her feet, he sheepishly suggested, his voice betraying his own disappointment in himself as he realized what little he could offer his family, while the turmoil was to soon unfold around us all.

He woke me early that morning before he left.

"But you won't be gone for long, will you, Papá?" I begged a question I already knew the answer to.

"I promise you, I won't be gone any longer than what is absolutely necessary. And now that I've made a promise to you, little lamb, you must also promise me something, that you will be a good girl for your aunts at the convent, who both love you very much." My eyes dropped, and I stared at my father's weathered hands and felt worry creep into us both at the prospect of my father leaving and that now I, myself, must leave home as well. "You must be very grateful for the education that your aunts were able to attain for you, dear. This is an opportunity that only the wealthiest children in Paris are fortunate enough to receive. It's only because of our family connections that your mother and I have found a means of having you enrolled."

I said nothing in reply. I knew how deeply my father cared for me, that his heart broke as much as mine did to have to separate our family. I also knew that the underlying reason for my going to the convent was to shield me as best he could from the shame our family was to endure. Paris was an unforgiving world for anyone, but even more so for a single woman trying to raise a daughter.

If only I could have told him then that his worries had little to be founded on. The convent was an absolute delight. My aunts adored me, and lavished endless love on me, taking great pride in providing me with the vital lessons that every girl must know in preparation of becoming a "good" wife. Each day was more wonderful than the last, and though my aunts were often times deeply concerned with my health, their letters to my father were constantly peppered with tales of visiting the circus with my classmates and reassuring promises of my recovering health.

While I was protected in the safe haven of the convent, my mother endured the worst of the storm alone. Nearly all of our assets were to be seized, and if it were not for our dear friend, Monsieur Tournehem's stepping in and rescuing her from financial loss and social humiliation, I don't know where we would be. She, too, was relieved to have me away from home while she endured the weight of these matters. But after one scary bout with my health during the winter, my mother couldn't endure having me away any longer, after all, three years had already passed with me in the convent. Finally, she was convinced that she had created a secure enough environment to take me out of the convent and bring me back home. So it was to be that come January, I returned to our home on rue de Clèry.

Another year had gone by, and I found myself happy and healthy, joyfully at my mother's side, and learning as much from her as possible. My mother was a woman of incredible resilience, courage and charm. Even as a child I could see how demanding and unforgiving the city was on a young mother, but she never faltered.

We wandered through Paris this chilly March morning. Every day felt like a discovery of a new part of Paris. We rounded a corner in a part of the city I had never been to before, and approached a thick wooden door, painted in a lacquer so dark that the wood nearly looked black. My mother reached for the bronze lion head knocker and tapped on the heavy wooden door. Moments later, a servant, her rounded face covered in countless wrinkles, opened the door just enough to see who was outside.

"Good day Adenorah, is she available?" my mother asked.

Turning, the servant led us through the corridor to a poorly lit room. I trailed no more than a step behind my mother, nearly clinging to the hem of her frock.

The candlelit room was so poorly lit that I had to rub my eyes so they would adjust to the darkness. Awaiting us sat a petite woman of a certain age. Her sapphire blue eyes were as clear as the sea, and her jet black hair was tightly pinned at the nape of her porcelain neck. She kept a black shawl with delicate rose embroidery draped dramatically to the floor as her posture rose proudly to show off her full height. Despite her strong features, there was a softness to her, an approachability.

I waited patiently in the corner of the room while she sat with my mother and spoke in hushed tones. I couldn't make out what they were saying, but I feared it had to do with the unfortunate situation my mother faced while my father was away. After a quarter hour, as we prepared to leave, this gypsy woman surprised us both. She stared, her eyes piercing through me, as though she were not looking at me but into me, and she ordered me to sit for a reading. Quietly, I looked to my mother who gently smiled and bowed her head in approval, and I obeyed. Sitting on the finely carved wooden chair, the gypsy stared intently at my hand, caressing the folds of my hand that seemed a lifetime younger than her own. "Perhaps," I thought to myself, "the woman has never had hands this young. Perhaps this gypsy has always looked just as she did now."

But of course she did indeed have hands as young as mine, at one time. Her story was so marvelously woven in with the flowers of Granada and the countryside of Andalucia, her beloved homeland that she had run away so far from, and now forbid herself from ever wasting a moment pondering on or longing for. She had been in love once. Only fifteen, young and beautiful, it did not take long for her beloved to ask her hand in marriage from her father. But the man whom her heart belonged to was a carpenter and very poor, and her father refused to allow his name to be disgraced by giving his daughter to someone so far beneath her own distinguished birth. Impetuous as young hearts tend to be, the two fled from home, escaping to Paris where they married. "I may never receive my family fortune, but love will be my riches," she often reminded her husband whenever he fretted over removing her from her family and the life she would have led should he have never entered her life. When her husband died that year of a fever, she refused to return to the family that abandoned her, and survived in the city using the only skill she had, her gift of fortune telling.

I looked up to find her penetrating eyes fixated on me.

"What is it, Madame Lebon?" came the concerned voice of my mother, fearing that what the fortune teller foresaw was something morbidly related to her young daughter's weak health.

Madame Lebon looked at me for a long moment, her eyes narrowing, taking in my childish features, and a smile spread across her hardened face, softening all her features. Standing behind my chair, I felt my mother's grip tighten, her breath held in fear of what omen was to be unveiled.

Finally, Madame Lebon, in a clear, resonating voice, announced, "You will reign over the heart of the King."

CHAPTER II

All the way home we walked in silence. My mother's mind was lost in thought as she considered such an outrageous claim. Her little daughter, the child plagued by frail health, was to reign over the heart of the King of France. She was absorbed in her thoughts, but I gave little credit to such an outlandish statement. Child though I was, I knew quite well that such a reality was impossible.

It was not until we finally returned home that my mother sent our servant to Monsieur Tournehem. She quickly scribbled a note, requesting that he "be so kind as to pay us a visit at his earliest convenience," which he would understand to mean that he must come at once. Upon his arrival, Monsieur Tournehem joined us in the salon. Here he found tea prepared and my mother and I awaiting his arrival. It was only moments before my mother pushed formalities aside and plunged into the matter at hand.

"You visited Madame Lebon with our *Reinette*?" he said, using my nickname. Monsieur Tournehem had always been very protective of me, and I could sense he didn't like the idea of my being there. "Well, at least you had a different reason to see her than all of her other clients. The city of Paris is still recovering ever since John Law and his outlandish promises of the riches of the 'royal bank.'" The banker, officially endorsed by the Crown, had convinced Paris to exchange their gold and silver for banknotes to be invested in Louisiana. A stock market formed and utterly failed, and all that had taken place not far from our little home.

"Thank goodness for the wise advice of our dear Pâris brothers. If it weren't for their disdain of John Law, I would have been as convinced as any other to give in to his ventures. Though I don't understand how they aren't able to make any progress in getting my husband home, after all, they have more influence and connections than most of the King's most trusted advisors."

"I'm sure they are doing what they can. After all, Pâris Montmartel is Jeanne's godfather, and his brother relies greatly on François' help. It's in all of our best interest that your husband return soon."

My mother's eyes dropped. She was one of those rare women that was truly in love with her husband, and despite the distractions of life's demands, she suffered from the distance between them. This was not how she envisioned her life.

"Of any matter, let's not talk of this any further," she said. "Charles, I asked you to come because I need your advice on Madame Lebon's prediction."

"But, my dear friend, that is quite impossible," Monsieur Tournehem chuckled. "The King is happily married and has blessed France with a new child nearly each year since his marriage to the Queen."

"Of course," Mother reasoned, "but their marriage is still young, and I am certain that, in time, he is sure to take a mistress. His Bourbon blood demands it."

"Naturally, you are right." Monsieur Tournehem conceded, he was always so agreeable. "But, Madame, consider that he is royalty, and our young *Reinette* is *bourgeoisie*. She would not even be allowed to be in the presence of our King."

My mother's dark brown eyebrows furrowed. "That does indeed pose a problem," answered Mother."Then, all of a sudden an answer occurred, softening her exquisite features. "But tell me this, has Madame Lebon ever faltered? Has she ever predicted anything that she was not absolutely certain of? No, she has not once faltered in her predictions, and I highly doubt this to be her first time."

Monsieur Tournehem sat quietly, staring out the window. "One cannot argue with that," he fairly admitted. "Let me stir on this matter for a while. This is a subject that mustn't be taken lightly." Leaning forward, he put down the cup of tea and gestured for the servant to bring him a glass of sherry, his preferred drink. Slowly, he exhaled, and lifted his eyes to look at me. "You do know I love this child like my own daughter, even more so as my beloved wife, God rest her soul, has left me no children of our own, and I have no inclination to marry again," he smiled sadly. "No need for any more children when I find such joy in your two. Jeanne-Antoinette and little Abel will be the only children I ever have. So I must warn you of the difficulty she will endure as a commoner in the company of nobility. It will only be the beginning of the insolence she is yet to experience at Court. She will be forced to tolerate the fanciful whims of Versailles, the cattiness, intriguing, and hypocrisy of Court gossip, and the ruthlessness of the ambitious courtiers who will by no means take kindly to a, forgive me my dear, but a middle class girl taking the place of their own. You do realize, if this is to become, she is to suffer constant hostility and competition, and my Jeanne Antoinette has too gentle a soul and sweet a nature to be poisoned by this environment that she will be forced to endure if she is to truly have any part in the King's life. Whatever misconceptions Paris has with the idealized world of the Court," he cautioned, "I assure you it can be a deceptively callous existence hidden behind a sparkling veil of regality, and I would wish to protect her from that world." My mother said nothing while these realistic concerns surfaced before her.

"Naturally you are correct; a more certain truth could not be told. Yet if this is to be her fate, to reign over the heart of the King…" I could sense my mother was leading Monsieur Tournehem to uncover what she wanted him to do without outrightly saying it herself.

"Then it is our duty to prepare her."

I spent the better part of the evening, sitting by the fire with Mother, pretending to read. But concentration was hopeless; my head and my heart were a whirlwind of questions and expectation. Who was this man whose heart I was destined to rule? Monsieur Tournehem declared that the King was happily married. I would never be his wife. But how could I dare be his mistress? I may have been young, but I knew myself well enough to know that it was against my nature to be anything but authentic, to say what I thought and how I felt. And what I felt was absolute certainty that I could neither be a mistress, nor joined to a man I didn't deeply and tenderly love. Am I to surrender my own dreams of a marriage of love for the petty satisfaction of being mistress to the King?

My mother always knew when I was troubled before I ever had to say a word. I could feel her eyes scanning my face.

"What is it, *ma petite fille?* Are you concerned about what Madame Lebon told us this morning?"

I sighed. "Mother, who is this man that I am to love?"

She told me of the story of an innocent child who was thrown into a tumultuous world; a mere babe, given an incredible amount of power and responsibility from far too young an age. His existence was played out in a glass house, visible for all to see and within reach of all, just as his grandfather, the great Sun King, Louis XIV, desired during his own reign. The gates of the palace were eternally open, people passing in and out freely. Such proximity to the royal household greatly pleased the previous ruler, yet this quiet young grandson would have much preferred his privacy.

King Louis XV had inherited the throne at the tender age of five years old, after a seventy-two year reign of his grandfather. Within a week's period, illness had struck nearly every member in his family, most likely scarlet fever. He was only rescued because his governess, the devoted woman he lovingly referred to as his *maman* Ventadour, sagely denied the doctor who had worked on and failed his parents, to treat young Louis. She instead took charge of his health, gave him a biscuit and some wine, and the two of them retreated to a safer haven. This simple remedy was the means of saving his royal life. If it weren't for her, he would have been at the whims of the chicanery of that obtuse doctor and perhaps joined the rest of his family in Heaven, and who knows what would have become of France. Thus the heavy weight of his new title as King of France lay squarely on his tiny shoulders.

So *maman* Ventadour had the great privilege of raising him for nearly two years by herself. Soon it was time for the young King to be taken under the wing of a governor. It was deemed more suitable for young King Louis to be taught how to lead the country than to indulge in the innocence of childhood. The change was too great, and almost immediately one could notice a marked difference in him. Separated from the closest thing he had to a mother, this handsome boy soon became secretive and withdrawn, much more introverted than before.

His governor, le Duc d'Orleans, Regent of France, made the executive decision, which naturally he had the power to do while Louis was too young to rule on his own, to move the child to the Tuileries

Palace. Most considered the duke's decision to be out of a desire to wield a more acute control over both the King and the nobles, whose privileged lives depended nearly entirely on the whims of their royal leader. The duke was well known for his remarkably strategic mind, but was also recognized for his ambition, and many cynically claimed that he had done this for his own selfish ends. But it wasn't actually true. The man had a sincere love for his Majesty, and constantly reminded him that the King was master, and he was merely a vassal to serve and suggest. The arrangement ended up working out quite nicely, and the only time that Louis ever came close to a notable objection of a suggestion by the Regent was regarding marriage arrangements with the tiny Infanta of Spain. But even in this matter, in the end the King willingly obeyed, granting that the Duke d'Orleans reasoning for the match was for the best of France.

And so, at the age of fifteen, he had developed into a charming, clever, brave and dashing young prince. There was certainly a shyness about him, however with nothing awkward about it, and all recognized him for his love and dedication to his God and country. And yet, instead of marrying a suitable bride and beginning to secure the future of France with a family with little heirs to the throne, he found himself committed to a five-year-old fiancée.

His betrothal to the young Infanta left the King of France in an unfortunate predicament. Because of the duke's insistence to marry the Spanish bride, Louis struggled between his profound commitment to secure the best interest of his country and the duty to rule his beloved people, whom he believed would be in a more secure country with the alliance with Spain. And yet, at the same time he felt completely humiliated at the fact that he was to be married to a child whom he couldn't even consummate the marriage with for another decade.

Soon the Duc d'Orleans realized the grave danger he had put his King and country in by this blunder. For it was a travesty to marry his Highness, the blood and heir of the fecund Henri IV, to a woman he could not be intimate with for years, thus removing the possibility of producing children of France. He also didn't consider that, if the King were to take a mistress at such a young age, the control that this woman, whom would surely be linked to (and a pawn of) one great family or another from Court, would potentially have over him, would be a grave threat. Europe had seen more than one reign undone because of the machinations of ambitious families that use their daughters to do their bidding.

Without an heir, the kingdom was in danger. Finally, it was agreed to send the darling little Infanta back to Spain and to find young Louis a proper wife. Despite the loss of her dowry, it was imperative that the King marry a princess that would succeed in her royal duty and produce little male Bourbons.

Ironically, Europe had few suitable royal brides to offer France at the time. And to make things all the more tangled, because of the ancient jealousies and intensely rooted rivalries between the noble houses of France, not one house would support another's candidate for the next queen. Nothing could be agreed upon, and no progress in the matter could be attained. Instead the King was to endure their incessant bickering.

Finally a princess was selected.

Hailing from Poland, the election of Marie Leczinska as the next Queen of France came as an utter shock to all parties, including the penniless bride herself. The woman could offer neither wealth, beauty, nor youth, but the pool of candidates was so limited that, of all options, she was the only one all could agree upon.

Nevertheless, the King adored her at once, for she was kind and regal, and very much welcomed in France, even more so as she immediately set to the task of producing little heirs to the throne.

This was the tale I was told of the man that I was to one day love. I understood his existence to be one of definitive boundaries and responsibility that prevented him from following his own heart. I wondered what he would do if he could choose, and to whom would he even allow himself to share his true desires.

CHAPTER III

In the epicenter of the French financial elite stood the Pâris Brothers and Monsieur Tournehem. These men were known to wield incredible power and influence, but as regular fixtures at my home since my earliest memories, to us they were simply family. It was with thanks to their excellent friendship and wise counsel my mother was able to improve our family fortunes. Home had a sense of stability again, and my mother seemed much more at ease knowing that her children would be cared for.

"Any word from your husband?" Joseph Pâris Duverney asked.

"His health is doing well. But François misses his children," said my mother. "It is so hard to be apart from him for so long." Her voice cracked at the thought of the time her husband was missing with his family. Few men delighted in fatherhood as my father did, and my mother lamented this time of his children's childhood that her husband would never get back.

"His absence is felt," Duverney concluded. He was rarely a man of many words, but what he said always resonated, speaking to the heart of the matter.

Monsieur Tournehem reclined against the ottoman, and my mother motioned for me to come sit beside her. "I hear our luck may be changing," he said, a smile spreading across his rosy-cheeked face. "Go ahead, Joseph, share with us the good news." Though Monsieur Duveryney was reserved, Tournehem loved to bring attention to him, especially when it was an opportunity for other's to acknowledge Duverney's goodness.

"Well, I don't want to announce anything quite yet," he said, leaning forward and looking at my mother, "but my brother and I think we have succeeded in arranging for your husband's return from Germany."

"No one could have finessed the situation better, my friend," declared Tournehem. "You see, little *Reinette*, I promised everything would work out just as it's supposed to."

My mother's hands covered her mouth, and tears gently rolled down her exquisite face. Monsieur Duverny handed her his blue handkerchief, and her eyes sparkled even more next to the color of the fabric. I hugged her closely, I knew she had been waiting so long for this day.

"In the meantime," Tournehem said, addressing me, "your brother and you will put extra practice into your studies."

I looked up from *La Princesse de Clèves*, one of my favorite books. I read it every year, and every year I understood more and more the complexity of the world of Court and the lack of satisfaction that one could find in marriage. I was relieved to know that I may not become a wife, but I would have even greater satisfaction because, unlike so many, I would truly experience love.

"Yes, *oncle*," I agreed. "I will do my very best, so that when Father comes home, he will be so happy when he hears how well I read."

With my father away for so long, there was even more pressure on my mother to raise my brother Abel and I. Monsieur Tournehem, having no family of his own, stepped in to take full responsibility of our upbringing as if we were his own children. He made sure we gained the education that he would have wanted for his own children.

"How are your lessons with Jèloitte at the *Comèdie Française* coming along?" he inquired.

"Very well. I am told I am learning quickly and he considers me to be a natural talent," I beamed.

"Excellent," he said, a smile making his cheeks look as rosy as apples. "Your education is of utmost importance, my dear. And you must know, nothing is too good for my *petite Reinette*. One could do no better than to learn under the tutelage of the exceptional Jèloitte. You can be proud of your education, I want you to feel pride in yourself," he stressed, and I knew he worried about me as a father worrying about the confidence of his child.

"Your mother tells me," he continued, changing the subject, "that you often ask about the King. If there is any recent new of him, you can be sure that I will always tell you. I know you are curious, darling, and you know you can always ask me about him."

"So you think what Madame Lebon said was true? You really do believe what she says?"

"Well," he began, considering his words carefully. "I am a man that prefers risks taken on calculated facts, so I hesitate to believe anything that isn't based on substantial information. But I must admit, that woman has a gift. She can see things."

"Is that why my education is so important to you?" I asked.

He patted my cheek. "Your and your brother's education would be important to me no matter what. I love you both so much, and you are so very clever, that it would be a shame to not encourage your learning. I may be conventional when it comes to fiscal matters, but I certainly believe in the unrivaled value of a broad education, and you can be sure I will expose you to as much learning as I can. But you are right, Madame Lebon's beliefs make your upbringing even more a concern. And when destiny presents itself, you will be ready. I will be sure of it," he said with a wink.

As time passed in this little circle of friends that moved in and out of the Court, I learned much about the happenings in the life of the King. Often, I stared at his image carved onto coins, or the portraits of him at our friend's homes, or the sculptures of him found in the streets. But I never asked. I was so curious to know more about him, but I always felt too silly to inquire to Tournehem or my mother about the King. It made me feel like the feelings that were developing were open for all to see, and it made me feel even more foolish for the words of a gypsy fortune-teller to carry such weight with me after all these years.

Finally I had the courage to speak to Monsieur Tournehem about him. "Years ago Mother told me," I bashfully approached the subject, "of the King's childhood. It was, by no means, a happy tale," I awkwardly tried to sound light-hearted, but truly I was searching for answers. "I felt very sorry to imagine the loneliness he must have endured as he grew up with no mother, no brothers or sisters to play with.

"As King, he had no equal to relate to."

"I cannot imagine not having Abel to play with, or my mother to talk to always about anything."

"Yes, but his is a unique existence. He is without peer, constantly revered as a demigod by all. With whom is he to share his innermost thoughts? Everything he says is noted, and the wagging tongues of gossip brings his every action and every reaction throughout the Court and into the newspapers of Paris."

"It's no wonder that he has gained a reputation of being withdrawn," I pondered.

"Well, it's not that he is necessarily withdrawn. When he is close with someone, he values their friendship very deeply. But he is very much a man that prefers his privacy. You can imagine how his reserved nature came as a shock to the Court of his grandfather. The Sun King seemed to take great enjoyment out of the attention he received. His reign, and the precedent he set for King Louis XV, was one in which the ruler of France is a public figure, visible to the world. It's like living in a glass house. Unfortunately, this grandchild of his is far from desirous of being such a subject of interest for the public."

"I couldn't imagine how he must have felt to have brides chosen for him, with little regard for who would be a match for him," I said. More than anything I wanted to hear of matters of the heart, and I hoped Tournehem would speak openly to me about it.

He smiled, aware of where I was attempting to lead the conversation. "No, queens are not selected by protective parents who have found the best potential match for their first-born son, as we will surely do for you. Queens are chosen after much deliberation by carefully chosen counsel members whose foremost thought is establishing a unity between the two countries for the best interest of the kingdom. But the Queen has done well for this country, she has done her duty and dedicated herself entirely to providing our patria with bonny princes and princesses to secure the continuation of their family and bring stability to the nation. She should be revered and honored," Monsieur Tournehem advised.

"If the Queen is beloved by the King, who am I to enter his life?"

"Because destiny has placed you there, and there will be purpose for you in his life. Another time we will talk more about the nature of the Court, it's a world far different than the one you and your mother live in. Then, you will better understand your place in his life." I didn't understand what he meant by that, and it left me feeling uncomfortable. "Until that time," he said, patting my little knee and putting an end to that conversation, "I will see to it that the education you and your brother are to receive leaves nothing to be desired."

And thus, my education was more acutely developed. My classes of singing, dancing and acting, instructed by Paris' celebrated Jèliotte of the *Comédie Française,* grew more frequent. The poet and dramatist Crébillon, whose life took an unfortunate turn with the loss of his young wife and the success turning sour after a number of failed plays acted out in Court, listened patiently for hours on end as I recited entire plays, which I was soon able to do by heart, as he gently corrected each and every error of diction. Pâris Duverney gifted me with what was to become my favorite instrument, the clavichord, which I practiced with as much dedication as enjoyment, morning and night. Meanwhile my mother, very much the green thumb, would take my brother and me outside and instruct us on the importance of botany and gardening, emphasizing the essential element of placement of each shrub and flower in creating an environment that stimulated all of the five senses. Drawing and painting were no more important of a skill set for an accomplished young lady than elegant handwriting and embroidery. I learned to ride and to even drive my own carriage, and of utmost importance, a skill that came quite naturally to me, was the art of entertainment and conversation.

And to complete the foundation of a proper education for a young lady, I was taught the chief significance of art. The Pâris brothers, as I found from their remarkable collection in their homes, were great patrons of the arts. The brothers had a taste for luxury, and an income that allowed them to acquire whatever they wished. Their rooms were filled with detailed tapestries, large collections of rare books and clocks, decadent chandeliers hanging low from the ceiling, and the finest furniture. Above all, they treasured their artwork the most.

The brothers took pride in collecting walls full of works produced by the most sought after artists. It was their affinity for art that fostered in me an appreciation for rarities that one often only finds in another part of the world, but also a value for the French artist. Of equal importance, in addition to their reputation as honest bourgeois with exceptional taste, they often impressed upon my brother and I that artists *must* be paid and patronized.

"France produces the finest artists in the world," they would say, "but the only means of a talented artist to survive is if his work is commissioned and paid for, and with the thriving of art came the thriving of culture. Little *Reinette,* it is our patriotic obligation to support them." I promised I would always do my best to help artists.

Therefore it was with a sense of duty that the Pâris brothers instilled in me the vital role both artists and patrons of the arts play in establishing an elevated society. This philosophy was all the more exemplified with the shameful little tales of the wealthy aristocracy who received their artwork but could never be bothered to pay for it.

At least once a week, Pâris de Montmartel would invite us all to dine at one or another of his exquisitely opulent estates. One day we might find ourselves at his home in the Marais, another at Brunoy or Plaisance. A man with an impressive appetite for a career he took great care in, he took equal pleasure in the leisure that his time at home offered him. Often he made a point of exposing me to the finer ways of his world, and shared with me the unrivaled collections of rare literature one would find neatly arranged in the high reaching ceilings of his library. Every aspect of his house was impeccably organized, everything had its place, and if ever one of us picked something up and set it down, he would adjust it to how it was sitting before. He was a man of great particularity, and had an attention to detail like I've never seen before. It was the same quality that made him so successful in his career.

After the heat of the day passed, he encouraged his guests to meander through his exceptionally maintained gardens. He had a predilection for botany, and housed some of the most exotic fruits one could find in France, including bananas and pineapples, that safely grew in his hot houses.

Other days, my mother would bring us to my favorite residence of all, Monsieur Tournehem's house in the charming countryside of

Etioles. The home was constantly being renovated, for Tournehem loved the novelty and creativity of architectural design. Often times he would inquire into my suggestion of how my brother or I might outfit the house if it were my own, and I knew such questions were yet another means to more acutely sharpen our own taste of style.

In short, every effort was put forth to develop me, as much as possible, into a woman of taste and sophistication, and I was grateful to *oncle* Tournehem and the Pâris brothers, and to both of my parents for investing in me and believing whole-heartedly in the relationship that was to unfold between the King and me, or in their words, my destiny. Nearly a decade passed in this delightful lifestyle, meanwhile not a detail of my education was overlooked and I grew into a woman raised with a single-minded purpose: to be worthy for the King of France. With this mission presenting itself in every aspect of my life, I began to believe myself ready to enter into this "destiny" of mine.

And then one evening, everything changed.

My mother and I joined Monsieur Tournehem one afternoon during a visit to Etioles. We strolled along the pathway and sat by the lake.

I pointed out the family of ducks swimming together, and how peacefully the sky reflected off the water. But neither Mother nor Tournehem seemed to pay any attention to what I said. I tried to break the silence, but neither of them answered more than a few words.

Such silence made me worry. They sat, as if absent-minded, with a pensive look on their faces. There was a palpable tension in the room, and I knew my mother was hiding something from me.

Finally I asked of any recent news of the King. The eyes of Monsieur Tournehem locked with my mother's and he quickly changed the subject to something we had never discussed before.

"*Reinette*, its time we discuss your marriage."

"My marriage?" I asked, completely caught off-guard. "But I have no desire to marry," I said, flatly. It didn't make sense. We had never spoken of any ideas of marriage before. My life, everything I did, was dedicated to the King. "Have I done something wrong? Are you punishing me?"

"Oh, my sweet child, no," my mother began, "of course you haven't done anything wrong."

"Then how could you propose for me to wed?"

My mother's voice grew firm. "You are eighteen; most young ladies are already married at such an age, and this cannot be delayed any longer."

"To marry a man I do not love?" I cried. "How can you say that? You, who has married for love, how can you want me to marry when I already love another! I want no one but the King. And he is already married, so if I marry, it only complicated things more, doesn't it. Besides, a husband would only be disappointed to find a wife who cares nothing for him, who only truly loves another."

My mother's voice grew stern. She was not pleased with the tone of voice I was taking with her. "The time has come for you to enter into society, and you cannot accomplish this without a husband. Until then, you will be perceived as a child and not be welcomed into polite company," she stated.

I sat quietly, not sure how to respond. My heart felt like it was lodged in my throat; my lungs felt like they couldn't fully inhale. I was to be married off, and to a man I didn't know and certainly didn't love. My entire life I was taught that I would experience true love. I was destined for the King, and I was willing to sacrifice the joys of being married so that I could find true happiness in love. I was privileged; I would be free from the condemnation of entering into a social contract that forced women into obedience with a man that hardly cared about, or even knew them, whose superficial purpose was the wealth or pedigree that the other brought to the marriage.

But now I was not to know such freedom and happiness as to be united with the one I loved. I was to marry. I would no longer be unique. I looked down at my beautiful satin gown, and at my hands gently folded over my gloves. I sat this way because that is how I had been trained to sit, because that was the style in which a woman was to behave. Everything I had done since my earliest memories had been for a purpose.

I had done absolutely everything possible to dedicate myself to narrowing this enormous gap that separated the King and me.

I was a young woman, eighteen; it made sense for us to finally find a means of meeting. No longer was I a child. Now was the time for me to gain his attention, not to marry another man and have yet another hindrance between us.

"I am no longer set apart. I am no longer made for a king. I am to be like every other girl: a bride, then a mother, then a widow." I had never felt more disillusioned.

"There's more that you must know. The King," she said, softening her tone, then, clearing her voice, "darling, I'm sorry but the King is in love."

CHAPTER IV

The next few weeks passed in a blur. I completely lost my appetite. Mother canceled all of my classes and appointments, politely explaining that I had come under another of my bouts with health. No one inquired further. No one need know it was my heart that was black, not my health. I refused company, I had no desire to see anyone.

My mother sat in the mornings by my bed, lighting the fireplace and reading to me.

"These curtains are always drawn closed in here," she scolded, clicking her tongue. "Darling, you need light and the healing freshness of air. Your health demands it."

She calmly walked over to the curtains draping down dramatically from ceiling to floor, and I noticed her beautiful golden hair, high cheekbones, and enchanting eyes. There was a sense of pride and a self-assurance that was perceptible in her reaching stature and in the natural elegance of her gate, and I envied her. Very few women I've ever met were gifted with the inner strength, beauty and resilience of my mother.

Our life had been so blessed that I often forgot the turmoil she found herself in, all alone, when my father had to flee the country and she was by herself with two young children. But she never faltered, and my father's faith in her was obvious. It was clear that she was a strength he could depend on; she was a survivor, and the foundation of my family. But of all her sacrifices, she refused to surrender love, and now she required me to.

All I could think about, all that mattered, was that the King was in love. Now should have been the time that we were to meet, the time that he fell in love with *me*. Surely the Pâris brothers could make an introduction. Surely something could have been done other than to find a wealthy suitor to marry me off to.

I couldn't bare it any longer. I needed to know who this woman was, the woman who took my place.

"Oh, hush. You haven't been defeated. Ambition and achievement of an endeavor are two different things dear, you must be more patient. Anyway, she is no beauty," my mother said flippantly, "nor is she known to be very romantic," she conceded. "But there is one thing that she has that few other women do. Louise-Julie de Mailly-Nesle, a *comtesse*, has been a fixture in the life of the King for ages, and it is for this reason, his comfort around her, that she has developed a relationship with him."

"Is it certain? How do we know it's not just a passing whim?" I pleaded, searching for just a little hope.

"She is acknowledged as his official mistress," my mother stated as a matter of fact. There was little more that needed to be said. I understood quite clearly that her reception of such a title signified her lasting role in his life.

I sat in a state of silence, my broken heart absorbing the details. "So I've lost him before we've even met," I said bitterly.

"Be at peace, Jeanne-Antoinette," Mother said, taking my hand in her own. "Timing is everything, and your time has not yet come. You have developed many talents, you are beautiful and full of life, a charm to everyone you meet, and you are kind and sincere. Though your father and I have little dowry to offer, any man will be honored to have you as his wife."

"That all matters little now," I said.

"Let me finish," she said, her soothing voice overcoming my impatience. "Even if you *were* to gain the attentions of the King, you would merely be a maiden to trifle with, you could certainly not stand on your own in his Court. At present, and despite what you may think, you are not yet prepared to enter his world."

"Then what is your instruction to me, Mother?" I cried, exasperated. "What is the wisdom that you seek me to understand? I am miserable. I cannot bare the thought of him with another woman, or the thought of myself bound to another man."

Placing her cool pale hand on my cheek and brushing the strands of hair off my brow, she went on. "I encourage you, do not be shortsighted and do not be anxious. You must establish your place in society, a society that was far outside of my own reach. But my limits will not be your own. You will be a force, a woman to be acknowledged and respected. Just as you see *les grandes dames*, women like Madame Geoffrin or Madame de Tercin, you too will be a woman to be greatly esteemed. Guests will be honored at receiving an invitation to your salon. And your name will grow outside of Paris, and into the mouths of Versailles," she declared.

"But I don't care about the grandeur of Parisian popularity, of being the subject of gossip. I'll never be happy with those trivialities, just like I could never be satisfied with the ostentatious lifestyle of Versailles. All I want..." I said, my voice cracking, and tears filling my eyes. I took a deep breath, fighting to regain composure. "My only wish is to feel the satisfaction of being loved by the only one I truly want."

"*Ma Reinette,* you have no need to tell me all this, I already know you've too noble a heart to be caught in the tangles of vanity or ambition. And I haven't forgotten about what Madame Lebon announced all those years ago. Don't worry, my dear girl, nothing has been in vain. Since we first discovered the relationship that you were to have with the King, it was not from a self-serving desire that I wished to see my daughter lifted to such lofty heights. Yes, your life with the King will be lavish, but we both know there is emptiness in wealth if it does not have love to sustain it. You and his Majesty are to love one another, and it will develop as naturally as breathing between you both. For you to experience this, that has been my single ambition in your upbringing. But his world and yours are deeply separated, so it is my responsibility to prepare you for the lifestyle that you will lead with as much dignity as refinement, so as not to make the King ashamed of the woman he loves. Therefore, you must marry, and marry well."

"And what of this woman, this *comtesse* that has taken my place?"

"As I always tell you, timing is everything, and your fate has not yet arrived," she smiled with assurance.

A marriage was easier said than done. My mother, try as she might, could not find a single man of reputable standing to accept a bride of my humble origins, of my parents scandalous past, or of the meager dowry that my family could provide. And yet, my dear Tournehem was unfazed at such difficulty. Instead, as a man of solutions, he readily suggested his nephew.

"It will be a splendid match," he promised. Tournehem had, he admitted, been quietly preparing for this moment in my life for quite some time. It was for this reason that he had made arrangements for the position of junior partner in Tax-Collection of Farms to be appointed to his nephew, Monsieur Charles-Guillaume Lenormand. He later deemed Charles to be his sole heir to Tournehem's wealth, which therefore meant disinheriting all other nieces and nephews. But he was only willing to secure his nephew into such a lucrative position on the single condition that the young man take me as a bride. To Tournehem, I was the closest thing he had to a daughter, thus making me the rightful heir to his empire. Of course, not everyone was pleased with this arrangement. My fiancé's father, Hervé Guillaume, was so disconcerted at finding a woman of such humble origins as myself as the match to his son's future that he wouldn't even attend the signing of our wedding contract.

A marriage of this nature meant I would be doing the one thing I had always thought impossible. Though I knew it would be impossible to marry the King, I somehow always imagined I would find unity with a man that I loved, just as my mother did. Instead, I was marrying a man that, ironically, was marrying me to secure his own financial future. But I refused to be like the other women. I refused to simply move from the watchful eye of my parents to the control of a husband. He was benefiting from this marriage as much as I was, and I would not be subjugated. It didn't matter that his family did not welcome me with open arms. They could look down on my humble social position, but they were smarter than to turn their nose up to the wealth that Tournehem offered through the marriage.

As for me, this would be no more than a necessary step towards my goal. Marriage would be a platform, and I would stand on it. I would stand on anything to reach for the love that I was destined for.

And so it was that on March 9, 1741, a beautiful spring day, my closest friends and family gathered to share in the celebration of this next chapter of my life as a wife. Monsieur Tournehem's niece, la

Comtesse d'Estrades, kissed me on both cheeks and welcomed me to her family, promising me that I would grow to be worthy of her family name. It was an odd comment, but I knew that it must have come from a place of friendship.

My mother fastened the satin buttons of my gown, the same gown she herself wore when she walked down the aisle so many years ago. She offered to buy me a new gown for the special occasion, but I was proud to wear what she wore, and to feel a sense of her strength on this day.

My father, who only years before had been able to move back home, placed my hand in the croak of his arm, and walked me down the aisle to my groom at the Church of Saint-Eustache. My fiancé took my hand, and I looked back at my mother. I wanted to feel the warmth of my mother's proud smile just once more before I crossed the threshold from childhood to becoming a woman.

CHAPTER V

In the world of the bourgeoisie, marriage did at times include elements of love and romance, though more often than not, the arrangement of a marriage was a business venture more than a union between two intertwined souls. Now more than ever, children of wealthy bankers and businessmen were married to members of the aristocracy that were faltering in their finances. This way, attaining a title of nobility become much more accessible, and despite the emotional emptiness that came with the prestige, parents promised the young brides that this way was best, and that eventually they would come to love their grooms.

I was fortunate. At first, it seemed that my husband simply agreed to a nuptial arrangement and he, in turn, could expect a life of leisure and wealth, eventually looking forward to inheriting a rather impressive fortune. And yet, as time passed, a friendship developed between us. I found him to be sincere, sensitive, kind, and very tender with me. My heart began to warm to him in a way I didn't expect. Certainly, there was nothing passionate about it, and my heart's demand for love remained, but for my husband I simply grew an affection and respect.

Just as planned, my husband and I moved into the marvelous estates with *oncle* Tournehem, including one on the rue Croix-des-Petits, which was located very near to my parent's home. We were catered to by servants, traveled about in horse and carriage, and worried about no financial obligations whatsoever. Tournehem still held his position as *farmer-general*, and my husband began working very closely with him. My parents and Abel visited us regularly, making this new chapter as a wife seem rather like an extension of my life before I was married.

With so many wonderful homes, I discovered a novel enjoyment into which Monsieur Tournehem encouraged me to indulge: design. We spent hours pouring over ways to renovate his estates and improvements that needed to be made. I pressed him on the art that must be acquired, and he allowed me to design garden paths that all led down to the stream, where soft blush pink roses led the way to lovely little row boats for a romantic ride along the water. All these enhancements would vastly improve the overall experience of the home, we both readily acknowledged, but most importantly, design was such a wonderful means of entertainment. And entertainment was my expertise.

As the Pâris brothers and the instructors of my youth impressed upon me throughout my upbringing, the arts were the height of entertainment. Acting was a pastime that was very dear to my heart, and something that I longed to exercise. No sooner did Monsieur Tournehem and I speak of this, than he insisted a theatre be built at Etioles. The theatre was outfitted in only the best equipment, and Tournehem warned me to not concern myself whatsoever with the cost, promising that this addition to the estate was an investment both financially and personally.

My life was changing quickly. Before marriage my energy was dedicated to educating myself. I was trained by those best in their field. I felt myself polished, prepared for the world. But entering into society challenged all that.

I may have learned from the best, but now, if I were to make any impact in society, I must put my education to use. Monsieur Tournehem often said, "Your charm, dear, it is your charm that captivates." And now that I could enter the social milieu, the stage he had built for me would become yet another platform.

There were few greater pleasures for me than acting. The entertainment I enjoyed from theatre was endless; I was able to delve into all kinds of activities that, together, created an incredible show. Here, I could lead in a way I hadn't ever experienced before.

All decisions were dictated by none other than myself. It was me who chose the fabric and design of each gown and every sash that my actors were to wear. I determined which plays we performed, and assigned each of my friends to the character best suited for them. Private theatres were all the rage in Paris, and our friends loved participating in them. It didn't take long before our performances became a regular activity. Soon, it was generally acknowledged that I was one of the most noteworthy amateur actors in France, and despite what I was willing to admit, I hoped my name would precede me and that somehow my name would reach the ear of the King.

Now that I was married and "out" in society, I was afforded the opportunity to partake in the singularly important pleasure of attending the salons of the fashionable Parisian women. Hosting a salon had become a pivotal role for women in Parisian society. In fact, the salon was one of the few places that a woman enjoyed power. It was here that the elegant ladies of the haute bourgeoisie welcomed the creative and talented minds of authors and artists into their homes, where nobility and intellect would intermingle and ideas were readily exchanged.

To host a successful salon was to be of the distinguished few whose names were spoken of often, even reaching the halls of Versailles, and this was exactly my endeavor. My name and reputation had grown enough that I was soon warmly received by the most exclusive of Parisian circles, and it was only a matter of time before I managed to establish my own salon and succeed in welcoming Paris' most influential to my home.

These select few involved a group that lived very much in the public eye. They were known as *les philosophes*, whose great minds and notorious names included those of Voltaire, Vauvenargues, Montesquieu, Marivaux, Fontenelle, and Helvetius. The stimulation from the exchange of these brilliant intellectuals, and there biting comments that resulted from the little jealousies that always exist between men of great talent, was unrivaled. Listening to their debates and discussions, I found myself as instructed as I was entertained, and yet, *les philosophes* argued that it was, in fact, themselves who were the more entertained. I laughed, knowing very well that they were pleased that I took a "modern outlook," as they put it, with the sometimes outlandish comments they said. And in turn, they appreciated my ability to "think philosophically," as opposed to the over-sensitive reaction they at times provoked.

I made sure to personally send invitations to the *grandes dames* of Parisian society, and I hoped that they would extend the same honor and invite me to their own salon. There was a Madame Geoffrin, a very kind and gracious woman of merit, who never failed to welcome me to her own salon on rue Saint-Honoré. Madame de Tencin was always invited, though she very sparingly allowed my mother and I the pleasure of joining her group. She was, I realized, ever so weary of any female rival. Madame du Deffand joined us often, as did the niece of Voltaire, Madame Denis. The young lady was dearly loved by her illustrious uncle, but to my great astonishment, paid him little mind.

I recognized that I felt content, and my life could easily go on in this manner, but in my heart I knew I wanted more. I refused to be complacent. Instead, I determined that every aspect of my life must have a purpose that ultimately led to the Court. If I was going to achieve what I had set out to, what I had put so many years into accomplishing, every action must be strategic. In order for my name to reach the ears of the King, it was imperative that I was known from Paris, and that my position in society was established.

It didn't take long before my name was always on the invitation list, and my husband and Tournehem proudly escorted me to and fro whatever party we attended. During one such soiree I was asked to perform. I sat on the bench in front of the clavichord and chose a song. As I finished singing, a woman with tears in her eyes, her face as sweet as the sunrise, placed her arms tenderly around me and hugged me.

"That was the most beautiful, the most touching performance I've ever heard." She said, squeezing my hand in her own, then dropping her eyes she walked away.

"That kind woman who hugged me, what was her name?" I asked Madame d'Estrades.

"You don't want to know," she cheekily replied, raising her eyebrows.

"Oh, do tell. I'm intrigued now."

"That," emphasized Madame d'Estrades, who always loved a good bit of gossip, "is Widow Mailly."

"The King's mistress?" I gasped.

Madame d'Estrades yawned, fanning her mouth nonchalantly. She loved being at the head of gossip, it made her feel superior. "Old news. The poor dear has been completely upstaged. Bore than she was, she made the foolish decision to constantly bring her much prettier sister to dine with herself and the King, and he, being a creature of habit, took a natural liking to the sister. One couldn't blame him, I hear their conversations were much more engaging, and of course it didn't take long until the royal mistress was quite forgotten. She only found out of the affair with the news that her sister was pregnant! Can you imagine the horror?" she said, satisfied with the salacious details she readily supplied.

I sat speechless, unsure of how to react, while Madame d'Estrades casually sipped her champagne. This tale was nothing more than entertainment of the royal liaisons for her, but for me, I knew that this easy dismissal and replacement could have been my own fate.

"Oh, but it gets better," she went on, her eyes widening with delight at unveiling yet more sinister gossip. "The new Mailly sister, after bearing the King a son, a royal bastard, died. It's a pity, after all her hard work of unseating her own sister. And this harmless creature, poor little Madame Mailly, is raising the child as her own."

"Thus receiving the nickname 'widow,'" I concluded.

"Precisely, and to her luck she is back in the presence of the King, dining privately with him on a regular basis, his consolation and friend as he mourns the loss of her sister and traitor. But I hear that silly woman has not gotten any wiser for the betrayal of her sister, for they say her other sister, much prettier and devilishly ambitious, has been seen frequenting their dinners. Surely it won't be long until the King takes a liking to a third Mailly."

CHAPTER VI

"I have a bit of information that you may be interested in knowing," my mother told me one very cold morning in February.

"And I have a bit of information that *you* may be interested in knowing as well," I replied coyly, hardly able to resist the wonderful news that I had been itching to share with her for days. "Mother, I'm going to have a baby!"

"Oh, darling, you could not have given me better news. I am so happy to hear that." She gushed, hugging me tightly. "Now you must remember to be very careful with your health. You have no idea how challenging it is on a woman's body to carry the weight of a growing child inside of you, and the stress that your body will constantly be under." My poor mother had been dealing with my frequent health issues since I was a child, and I knew this news would worry her nearly as much as it delighted her.

"I haven't told a soul. I wanted you to be the first to know."

"I am truly honored. Oh, a grandchild, what a wonderful surprise. I am just overjoyed. My darling *Reinette*, you could not have made me happier." Then, she began to plan. "Now we must tell your father and brother, and you must not forget to tell Tournehem and the Pâris brothers right away. I'm sure they will feel this little child is as much theirs as it is yours," she laughed. "Jeanne Antoinette, I cannot tell you how happy I am. My greatest joy in life has been being a mother to you and Abel, to watch you grow and experience life, and all the beauty this world brings. And now you get to experience the same."

"Thank you Mother. I can only hope to be as devoted and loving of a mother as you have been to me. Now, what news do you have?"

She smiled, staring into my eyes and feeling the satisfaction of the moment. She sat down next to me, and placed her hands on mine. "Your name has reached the ears of his Majesty, the King, and has caused quite a stir."

"How so?"

"Do you remember the night you played the clavichord? Well, from what I've heard, your name was first mentioned by Madame Mailly after listening to you play. Apparently she was deeply touched by your music, and upon returning to Versailles, she spoke of you at Court. She had very kind things to say, even conceding that you are a young lady of unrivaled talent and charm."

"She is very gracious to have given me such a compliment, it's a shame that everyone now refers to her as Widow Mailly, the poor thing."

My mother disapproved of the nickname. "Anyway, as you know, your cousin, Sieur Binet, is in the King's service. It was him that made the connection, explaining that you are the women Madame Mailly was referring to. He said that the woman who has no equal in her talent of the clavichord is the same woman who the King often times sees driving her own blue phaeton dressed in a pink gown in the Forest of Sénart. Sieur Binet let it be known that you are his relative, and agreed with Madame Mailly that you are as lovely as you are talented. Well, you can imagine that it was only a matter of time before the word spread through the Court that the King has taken notice of you."

My mother was beaming, but I couldn't imagine how she wasn't concerned about the conflict of timing.

"But I would venture to guess that this news makes little difference," I reasoned, shaking my head. "Mother, don't you see? There could be no worse timing for his Majesty to take notice of me. I am pregnant, and soon to become a mother."

"Sometimes, when we face multiple conflicts at once, they counterbalance each other," she replied, her voice perfectly calm. "Yes, I see that you are pregnant, and the timing could not be better. You see, you were not only noticed by the King, but by his new mistress, the third Mailly sister, Marie-Anne de La Tournelle, as well, and she cares very little for the fact that your name is on the tongues of the courtiers and that the King has become aware of you."

"How can you expect that I am to now gain the attention of the King and then to eclipse this Marquise de La Tournelle with a growing baby in my belly. I am no rival to the established mistress in this state."

"But you are mistaken. This news comes as a warning as well as a gift, for the timing could not be more perfect. A fortnight after the conversation with Madame Mailly and Sieur Binet, the Duchesse de Chevreuse happened to mention your name in the presence of the King. Well, the Marquise promptly stepped so forcefully on the foot of the Duchess that the poor woman nearly fainted! I am told that the next day, the Marquise de La Tournelle called on the Duchess to apologize for her little violent act of jealousy. She excused her violent little reaction as a fit of jealousy, admitting that she knew that there have been designs "to give you to the King," as she put it. She also knew that you and the Duchess have been friends since childhood, and made clear that you are not to be seen in the hunt again. That is a warning that I would dare to heed."

"So, how is this news a gift?" I asked sarcastically.

"The timing could not be more perfect," she repeated. "The King has taken notice of you. His Mistress, who they say he is desperately in love with like never before, is clearly threatened by you. At present you have no freedom to enter the sight of the King in your condition, but the fact that he knows of you brings an air of familiarity to you. When the time comes for you to meet, he will not only be familiar with your name, but more importantly, intrigued by you – a woman he has heard so much about but has yet the pleasure of knowing. What perfect timing to bare a child! Don't you see, fortune has smiled upon you."

"Mother, I do not doubt your foresight, but consider that after pregnancy and giving birth, all that time spent away from the King, his mistress is only gaining more control in his life and a greater permanence in his heart. If I have his attention now, then it is now that I must act. But my hands are tied! Really, I am missing the first chance that I have at meeting the King."

"*Ma Reinette*, how many times must I remind you, do not underestimate the importance of timing, and it is in your favor. You do not know what is to come next. You worry that time is running out, and are anxious to have your opportunity with the King now. But remember what Madame Lebon saw in your future and have patience for your fate to approach you. Trust me when I say, what you consider an inconvenience today, is a gift tomorrow. Now is not the moment that you will enter the heart of the King, but that moment is indeed approaching."

I knew her logic was dependable, and trusted her wisdom. But I couldn't help but be agitated at the situation. The more time I spent with my husband, who just adored me, and doted on me even more now that I was carrying his child, the more our friendship developed into love. How many times I've told him how happy he makes me, promising that I would never leave him, unless of course it was for the King. He would laugh light-heartedly, thinking it was only a joke, then would take me on his knee and kiss me. Our life was enjoyment and happiness. Or at least, it was easy and calm. That is more than most could ask for.

And yet, I felt in my heart that destiny was propelling me to something outside of this simple life. I was sure that Madame Lebon's words rung true, and it would only be a matter of time before they did. And if this were the case, the life I was creating with my husband, and the little family we were growing together would be shattered.

Then I considered the opposite. What if I were to never meet the King? What if our love was never to unfold? My life now would continue as it is, with theatre and salon and soirees and all these lovely pleasantries. But would there be something missing? Would I be giving up the great love, the passion that brings meaning and purpose to life, in order to protect the world I had cultivated?

CHAPTER VII

These months of pregnancy came and went with great difficulty. My mother was right in her concern for my health. It wasn't that I couldn't get pregnant, it was that I perhaps shouldn't. Women with stronger health than my own died everyday from childbirth, and this was my second pregnancy.

My first pregnancy was very difficult as well, and I gave birth to a beautiful son. I could feel the pride beaming in my husband's face when they announced that a son had been born, and even now I do not forget the grief we both felt together at the loss of our first child's life in early infancy. So this time I took extra care of myself, going into confinement months before the child was expected, rarely leaving our home, and instead welcoming the many guests that would come and visit for an afternoon or for supper. I could not exhaust myself with my participation and organization of theatre. Instead, my time was spent practicing my instruments, painting, writing letters to friends and relatives, and reading poetry aloud to the baby – anything that created a calm, peaceful environment.

The last month of my confinement found me spending my time entirely in my bed. Both my body and my mind were utterly exhausted, and my mother made sure that visitations be limited to only family. Though we had servants, she insisted to be the one that brushed my hair, rubbed my swollen feet, and read aloud to me. My husband spent time with me throughout the day, but I had such little energy and could offer him no entertainment. He spent no more than half an hour with me, informing me of any news in Paris, then would rise and carry on with his day. But my mother was always by my side, hardly leaving me alone for a moment. I was so grateful for her calm presence, her understanding of what I was experiencing, and her confidence that I was much healthier this time around.

It was only a week later that my beautiful child, my little Alexandrine came into this world. She was adorable in every way. She had the softest porcelain skin and blushing little cheeks, with heart-shaped lips and grey eyes, just like mine. And best of all, she was strong and healthy.

My whole world stopped the moment this child entered my life. From the moment the doctor pulled her from inside of me and laid her on my chest, I knew I belonged entirely to her. Never had I before felt such a bond. I felt a love that was so profoundly deep, so all-encompassing for this little girl, and I couldn't help but stare into her beautiful little face and hold her to me for hours. Every moment was precious, and I knew this time with her was all too fleeting. I promised to raise her with the same love and dedication that my mother had afforded me.

My entire family was equally as enchanted with this darling little creature, and no one more than my father and *oncle* Tournehem. They both adored her the moment they laid eyes on her, so much so that a stranger wouldn't be able to tell which was the grandfather and which was the friend. Time united these two gentlemen like brothers, and they felt that they had both equally become grandfathers. I watched with satisfaction while one would hold little Alexandrine and rock her, their eyes never moving from her sweet cheribum face. Soon enough, the other would offer to relieve the firsts arms and hold the child himself, and they would go on and on taking turns with their grandchild.

My child was born, a beautiful healthy girl, and my heart could not be more full. Yet my health was not strong, and my mother insisted that I take time to recover.

My mother sat quietly in the chair by the cradle and read the letter she had just received from Pâris Duverney. I paced the room, gently rocking little Alexandrine in my arms, and listening to the sweet little baby sounds she murmured. I looked up at my mother to find her lips tightly pursed, her eyes cast down and lost in some distant world. It was an expression I rarely saw on her, a face solemn with concern.

"The King, he is ill," she said, looking up at me. She placed the letter on the desk and looked out the window.

"How badly?"

She exhaled slowly, and I could tell she was choosing her words wisely. "I dare not say." She took the baby from my arms and placed her in the cradle.

"Mother, please. I must know," my voice cracked. "How is the King?"

"It is rather dire," she began, handing me the letter to read for myself. "At first, he was only taken slightly ill, and brushed it aside. After all, he is on campaign with the troops, and since he is known to have always been as healthy as an ox, he paid it no mind." The King had only just arrived earlier at Metz, near the Rhine in August. He'd gone in an effort to support the army. "Duverney writes that a fever came without warning and only now the King realizes how serious the threat is. Darling, it has become so grave that there have been discussions of the Last Sacrament."

I gasped aloud, covering my mouth with my hand. "Have they bled him?"

"Yes, of course. His doctors have bled him and purged him, but it has all been to no avail, and most probably only weakened him more." She crossed her arms and looked back at me. "Pâris-Durverney writes that the Duc de Richelieu took full advantage of the King's weakened state. As soon as he realized that the King's life was now in danger, he took charge, and will allow no one into the royal chamber. He is using this as a means to exercise his own superiority over other courtiers," she said, shaking her head in disapproval.

My eyes darted up from Duverney's letter. "The Marquise de la Tournelle, the King has ordered for her and her sister to be sent away!" I said, astonished.

"The King's mistress is no longer a marquise," my mother corrected. "Just recently she received the title of Duchesse de Châteauroux."

"But she will be sent away, then?"

"It is even more concerning if she is. If it is truly feared that he will not survive, the King will have no choice but to send her away. Anyway," she said, returning to the letter, "Durverney says that the Queen and Dauphin must be sent for, and a confession is to be made by the King. For measures as alarming as these to take place, I am sure that everyone is preparing for the worst."

Streams of tears ran down my cheeks, and I felt like I couldn't breathe. My King, my beloved's life was in danger. I felt overwhelmed with fear. My body began to cramp up, and I collapsed on the bed.

My mother never left my side from that moment, ensuring that her daughter was not to endure this pain alone. She read to me from the Bible, and though we had never been religious, it was only in prayer that I found any solace. The Lord would keep our King alive, I told myself. Where medicine might fail, God would not. France could not endure the loss of Louis XV. I could not endure the loss of the man I was created for.

My health grew weaker over the passing weeks, the head aches more frequent and severe, and I lost all appetite. My mother encouraged me to eat, for I had a child now, a child whose life depended entirely on me.

My only peace came from the letters that Pâris-Durverney knew I depended on. Each one brought the possibility of hope that the King had recovered, but they only grew more worrisome. It seemed that the Duc de Richelieu had done his best to ensure that the few visitors that were allowed into the King's chamber assure him that this was nothing to worry about and promised him that his health was sure to be restored in only a short matter of time. But it was impossible to keep up the rouse. His Majesty's condition had become quite dire, and as much as the Duc de Richelieu meant to shield him from the truth, there was no way of denying it.

The time had come for his confession and to receive the Last Sacrament. The Bishops of Metz encouraged the King to also make a public repentance, and it was required that he remove his mistress and her friends from his party. For a man as proud and shy as the King, I could only imagine his embarrassment at having to perform a public repentance.

It took only a matter of days before we received Pâris Duverney's following letter. To everyone's horror, instead of leaving as she was ordered to do, the wretchedly ambitious Madame de Châteauroux and her sister disobeyed the King's order and stayed in a home located not far from Metz. Her great ally, the Duc de Richelieu, invited her to stay there, at his residence. Richelieu feared that if the King was separated for too great a length of time from his mistress, she would lose her strength of influence of him or be replaced. The threat of a shift in power affected the mistress just as much as it did the duke, and he was resolved in protecting his position of influence with the King, and his superiority at Court.

Every action at Court was like a chess game of manipulation that each courtier must play to survive and to thrive, and it was all at the expense of the King. I couldn't imagine how he could ever trust anyone's opinions, knowing full well that every suggestion came with hope of a favor or as a means of benefiting one's family. And now, because of the disobedience of the duke and the King's mistress – two people he was closest to - the bishops of Metz and Soissons refused to attend to the King at the moment he needed the relief of a clear conscience.

The Queen and the Dauphin arrived in great haste. The few courtiers that were privy to the happenings between the royal family mentioned that the King was very tender with his wife, apologizing with great sincerity and begging her pardon. Most were even surprised at the great affection he showed towards his son. More affectionate, it seems, than what would be expected from a dying young King that is staring at the man who will be replacing him. But the King loved his family dearly. At heart he was truly a family man, and he spoke to his son not as a ruler, but as a father.

I will not attempt to convey my profound dismay at the threat of losing the King. I will only say that my health has never been so weak, or my own life so greatly disregarded as at that moment. I wished to God that I could exchange the remainder of my years for those of the man I had been created for. I would have gladly given up my life to save his.

Only two days later, the manservant entered my chamber to announce the arrival of Madame d'Estrades, who promptly strut into the room in her usual attention-grabbing manner. It was only after taking note of her midnight blue gown draping luxuriously to the floor, with pearls sown along the sleeves with impeccable attention to detail, that I realized how little regard I had for my own appearance at the moment.

"You could not imagine the scandal that happened at church today!" she announced, before taking in my present state. "First we will order tea, or perhaps something stronger. *Ma amie*, you look frightful."

"I see you were in attendance for the society and not for the sermon," I half-heartedly teased, acknowledging full well that my dear friend cared little for the moral enlightenment the priest tried to instill in his congregation.

"But you are mistaken, for I have never heard a sermon that has roused such interest," she said, sitting herself down in the cream satin lounge and removing her cap, I could see she was inspecting the floral detail of the cushions and wondering to herself if they were to her taste.

"I must admit," I said, sitting back as they served me tea, "a bit of intrigue is much needed in my state."

"I'm glad to hear it," she replied, scanning me once over. "Truly, I have never seen you look so wretched," she said, squeezing my hand between hers. "It pains me to see you thus."

"Well, life is much easier to endure with your company. Now tell me, what gossip have you to cheer me today."

"You won't believe it when I tell you, it's *that* appalling, and I cannot imagine what in the world those blundering bishops of Metz were thinking." She dropped her eyes and inspected her well-groomed nails cavalierly, though she knew she now had my full attention the moment she spoke of Metz.

I sat patiently, knowing full well that she loved to play this little game of bearing news she knew was important to her listener. Madame d'Estrades savored this fleeting moment of power and anticipation.

"The confession, the one that those thoughtless bishops extracted from the King when he was in his worst state, has been made public, printed in newspapers and handed out to every parish in France. Every preacher in the country has been galvanized by the scandal, making it a point to have the confession as the chief subject of their sermon. Every one of them are all expounding relentlessly on the abject sinfulness of adultery," she scoffed. "You would not believe the sensation it's causing. Why, all of Paris is outraged!"

"My God," I was astonished. I could only imagine the King's mortification. "How could they have ever degraded him in this manner in front of his own people? Couldn't they have allowed this matter to remain private?!"

"Precisely, it's complete pandemonium. Everyone is aghast at the shock of bringing this to the pulpit. You wouldn't believe it, people are in an uproar, crying in the streets, holding each other, and speaking of their "*Bien Aimé*," their beloved young King."

"This should have remained a private matter," I repeated, shaking my head. "The royal family has endured enough. The King's life has been in danger, and now, a terribly sensitive, utterly personal matter made to be a topic of public debate."

"And you mustn't forget about that sinister Madame de Châteauroux. She's the cause of all this embarrassment. I'm sure the entire royal family is affected."

"Don't remind me. Just the thought of that horrible woman upsets me."

"You know," said Madame d'Estrades, leaning forward and enjoying the telling of gossip, "upon her return to Paris, she was pelted with eggs and hissed at. In fact, I heard she was nearly lynched for having almost impeded the King from receiving the Last Sacrament! The Parisians loathe her, anyone could certainly understand why. But she is a dangerous thing; she has made clear that she is not one to be trifled with. You can count on her taking her revenge on anyone trying to cross her, even now during her disgrace."

"My dear, thank you for sharing this with me, but I don't believe I can bare much more. The King's life is in danger, and now his legacy is tarnished. Please excuse me, but I must rest."

"I am so sorry, Jeanne-Antoinette. I did not mean to upset you. I should have thought wiser than to come now to share such distressing information," and her words were sincere. "Now, tell me, how is the child?"

"Alexandrine is wonderful. She is strong, and healthy, full of life and animation. You can imagine how charmed everyone is with her."

"I am sure she is just as delightful as her beautiful mother." Madame d'Estrades kissed my cheek, and bid me farewell.

"He must live," I whispered, and stared at the crackling fireplace. "The King must live. He will recover. And when he does, I will be there."

"Jeanne-Antoinette," my mother woke me early one December morning. "Jeanne, wake, my child. We have news from Pâris Duverney." She folded back the satin sheets, her cool hand brushing back my hair. Then looking at my eyes swollen from tears and the tissues carelessly tossed next to the lovely Chinese porcelain water pitcher. "Darling," she gently scolded, "you must wear your rouge, you cannot be bouncing around the house like a maid. Where is your pink gown with that superb lace that you just finished having made?"

I couldn't care less about lace and rouge. "Mother, please, what news?" and she could hear the anxiety in my voice.

"The kind that it is worth sitting up for. The King has recovered."

"Oh, praise God in Heaven, the King is going to live," I gasped out loud. I felt the satisfaction of air filling my lungs, and sat up straight to exhale. It felt like the first time I could breathe deeply since this whole Metz affair began. My mother wrapped her arms around me, holding me tightly. She knew that not only did this letter bring with it news of the King's recovery, but the recovery of her daughter's health as well.

"As do I. He had just recently returned to Versailles, and it's been confirmed that his health is restored, even through this horrible winter we are having, and he is strong as ever," she paused, eyeing me. "Of course, his immediate next act was to call upon the return of his mistress."

"I see," I said, looking down. "I had the silly hope that after she was sent away from Metz, she would not be returning to Court. Of course, I knew better." The King is a creature of habit, and it was only natural that he would not forget about the woman he loved.

"Yes, he sent for her directly, very repentant of ever having sent her away. The duchess, the furious creature, demanded that she first receive a formal invitation from none other than the Compte de Maurepas. She knew very well that he had been intriguing against her for quite some time, and this was her foolish form of displaying her dominance and place of power above his own."

A foolish move, indeed. "That seems unnecessary to make this horrid situation all the more uncomfortable. If she truly loved him, she would have been grateful for his recovery. I imagine it has only caused the King all the more anxiety to deal with the squabbling disputes of his mistress and chief advisors."

"Certainly. I am glad to see you have found the lesson in his previous mistress' mistakes. Her request was one of selfishness, and will only serve to further complicate the relationship between the King and his advisors."

"Mother, what do you mean, his *previous* mistress?"

"Patience, let me finish," her eyes smiling at what she was about to reveal. "This all happened just a few days ago, on the twenty-sixth of November. The Compte de Maurepas obeyed the King's command and left at once for Madame de Châteauroux's home on the rue de Bac. I imagine she could not hide her feeling of triumph over him and everyone else that had hoped she would never return to Court. The duchess made it known that the compte was to submit to her, that her influence was officially greater than his and he must now come to terms with that and submit to her position of authority. But her claims of superiority got the better of her. In no more than twenty-four hours she developed a horrible fever. Many suspect it to be an act of poisoning from the Compte de Maurepas, though I very much doubt it was his doing. Her fever worsened over the next few days, as she lay in her bed, delirious with pain. Jeanne-Antoinette, his mistress is dead." Squeezing my hand, my mother announced, "*Ma Reinette*, your time has come."

CHAPTER VIII

"My time has come." The words rang in my ears. With these words came the hope that now was my opportunity to finally find my way into the presence of the King, to see if the prediction of Madame Lebon rang true, or if I was just another pretty face, another of the wives of his subjects that was madly in love with the dashing thirty-four year old King. But I knew how different from these others I was. There was a sincere love in my heart, and I would have to prove myself the exception from the rest. The largest obstacle preventing my having already met the King was now gone, God rest her soul, but I was certain that many more hindrances lay squarely in my path.

The King was profoundly heartbroken. He and a very small group escaped to Trianon, but disaster followed him there. *Maman* Ventadour, his governess who raised the young orphaned King with all the love and tenderness of a mother, had passed away. In only a short period of time, the women whom he loved most had been forever taken from his life. The impact of such a shock must have been crushing, and he could not rest at Trianon any longer. He and his closest circle took flight to the hunting lodge in La Muette.

My health, having fully restored, allowed me the great pleasure of strolling through the garden of our home at Etioles with my dear Monsieur Tournehem. After what felt like too long of a separation from society, I was glad to have him fill me in on all the latest news of the city and what he had most recently heard from the Pâris brothers of the war. Monsieur Tournehem amused himself just by talking, and loved having an audience.

I tucked my hand into the crook of his arm. "Do you think the King will return to the Queen?" I asked, directing the conversation to what I wanted most to learn about.

"What makes you say that, dear?"

"Well, he really is such a family man, and I'm sure this whole Metz affair has left an impression on him," I said, thinking of how embarrassed the King must have felt after the disobedience of a mistress and the recalcitrance of the priests. "It makes sense for him to return to his family."

We walked on in silence for a long while.

"As much as some might consider that to be the right thing to do, I highly doubt that it would be probable of the King to return to conjugal life."

"But it seems to me that he is a very religious man," I pointed out, thinking of his refusal to attend to his Easter duties, or even to take communion. Despite his family and the Church's frustration, the King would not take communion while living, as he saw himself, as an adulterer. He refused to make a mockery of his religion by confessing when he knew he was not going to change his ways. Although many would have preferred that he followed the course of the kings before him and perform the ceremonious rites of the King, I respected his conviction and refusal to act like a hypocrite to please others. "I'm sure he would feel relieved to take communion and fulfill his religious duties as king, and he will only allow himself to do that if he returns to his wife, the Queen."

Monsieur Tournehem patted my hand and smiled at me. "It would certainly be a wonderful solution, dear. The Queen suffered much abuse from Madame de Châteauroux. She had a reputation for taking pleasure in mocking the Queen and making a display of the little influence the Queen held. I'm sure it upset the entire royal family. Unfortunately, the King has had a mistress in his life for so long that the Queen is now used to another woman fulfilling that role. Her Majesty has succumbed to the leisure of middle age and, I suspect, has no intention of stepping into the role that his mistress has fulfilled. She would leave his entertainment and romance to another, and continue in her pious duties and games of cards. Why, even her father says that when the King is with her, he yawns like at Mass. But you must understand, she has been conditioned to accept that the nature of the life of a queen includes a mistress, and I doubt she is prepared to change her habits at this point."

We reached the edge of the river. The sun was behind us now, and would set soon.

"Do you think he will take a mistress immediately?"

"I do," he continued, "the world keeps turning, and the Court carries on. The position of *maîtresse en titre* remains available, and is one of the most enviable positions there is. It is an unrivaled opportunity to influence the King, and I have no doubt that there is no shortage of subjects who have a duchess or two to suggest," Monsieur Tournehem concluded.

"He is rarely without a mistress," I conceded, acknowledging it as a matter of fact.

Tournehem chuckled. "It's true, he does not like to be alone for long. But he is a king, and more than a king, for his Majesty is the King of France. You must remember, Jean Antoinette, that his grandfather, the Sun King, was one of the most lustful men in France. If his mistress took too long to undress, he would sleep with her maid before he satisfied himself with his lover. But his people were proud of his lustfulness. For them, it represented a sign of French vigor.

"Did Pâris Duverney say if there is someone that's already caught the King's attention?" I asked, hoping to mask the worried tone in my voice.

"No one in particular, but there is little doubt that his courtiers are losing no time in preparing fresh candidates to take the place of the Madame de Châteauroux. The Duc de Richelieu, who perhaps has the most influence of all, has yet another Mailly sister, among a number of other beautiful and well-bred nobles. I've even heard the women of Paris talk of becoming his mistress. Everyone knows that taking the title would be an incredible privilege that would bring enormous wealth to their family. I'm sure you've heard tails of the Vallière family, or the Gramont family, and how they have amassed a fortune and rose high in power, simply through affairs with kings."

"Exactly, there are dozens of more beautiful women with more access to the King and of better pedigree. Who am I to even consider that he will take any notice of me?" I begged.

"The King may be a man of habit, but he is also a man of great intelligence. I can only imagine he has lost his taste for these aristocratic women taking advantage of him. Their ambition and greed must have bored him by now. I would think," he said, turning to me, "that the King does not desire another countess or duchess pushed upon him by one of his subjects looking for advancement in power and wealth. This leaves him with one option, a bourgeois."

We turned and walked in silence back towards the house.

"And I would have thought that would have made my sweet *Reinette* smile. So then, child," he said, like a father, "tell me what is it that is troubling you."

"I do not want to dishonor the Queen. I want so badly to be the one that the King chooses. But I worry that taking the place of Madame de Châteauroux would only cause her more shame."

"That noble heart of yours. Darling, you may be the only woman that will ever enter the King's life that would ever consider the feelings of the Queen. The simple fact of the matter is this: there will be another mistress. And if it is to be that you are to enter into the King's life, both the King and Queen are better for it. You see, the King has a romantic nature and will succumb to the will of his *maîtresse*. She will wield her influence to perform favors for her friends, and this sense of power often times allures a woman that seeks superiority instead of love. If the Queen has so little influence, why should a mistress go to any great lengths to please her? But you are not like those others that clamor for power. No, my sweet girl. You are unique from the rest, for you will love the King truly and ask nothing in return. You will show great respect for a queen who has been treated so poorly by the entire Court."

I smiled and hugged him tightly. "I suppose the only question now is, how do we meet?"

CHAPTER IX

How to gain access to the King? It was the one question that every woman in Paris and Versailles had been dying to know since the death of his wretched Madame de Châteauroux. The King was known to frequent masquerades and balls, but it would be impossible to meet him there. As soon as his identity was known, he would immediately be surrounded. I could perhaps ask my cousin, Sieur Binet, to make an introduction; I knew he had many moments alone with the King and could easily bend his ear. But that's what any woman would do, and it lacked originality. However we met, I knew I wanted the moment that we first met to be magical, unforgettable.

There were so many restrictions that limited anyone, particularly anyone that was not of noble birth, to be presented to the King. Still, I was determined to find a way. Christmas had come and gone, and there was no rumor of the King having taken a new mistress. But I held no false illusions. Time was of the essence. I needed to act.

The King and his Court lived a transient lifestyle and were constantly moving from one place to another. After a period of time, he grew restless at staying at Versailles, and it was an established routine to travel with his entourage to his royal chateaus. So just after the New Year, the King left for Choisy.

This was my chance. There could be no greater opportunity. Sénart was one of the King's favorite hunting grounds, and I knew the forest like the back of my hand. There could be no more perfect place to gain his attention and to successfully stand out.

That morning I rose before the sun. Every detail of my beauty routine seemed even more important than usual, everything required extra care, because today I was determined that the King and I would meet. I concocted a mixture of egg yokes and honey to set on my face for an hour, just as my mother taught me to do. Next, I applied rose water before powdering my face and adding a rose-pink rouge to my lips. The night before I laid out my favorite gown of sky blue that most complimented my grey eyes and my figure. The horses were to be groomed and prepared, and the pink phaeton was to be polished. No detail was to be overlooked. Today I must sparkle.

I considered what time I could expect to encounter the King. Most probably, he and the others would have been hunting since daybreak, so I left just before noon. My horses knew this trail well, and it took very little effort to lead them. I straightened the fabric of the skirt of my gown and adjusted the lace cuff. With the realization that this moment was the beginning of the rest of my life, my heart raced faster, and I hoped the King would be impressed at the sight of a woman, unaccompanied, driving her own phaeton.

I could hear the hearty laughter of men as I rounded the bend in the road. Resting in the clearing, surrounded by dogs barking and jumping about, I found a troupe of men reclining on logs or against their horses. My heart beat violently in my chest, I felt like I could hardly breathe. "Inhale slowly," I told myself. "Regain your composure." My eyes searched with more anticipation than I'd ever felt before. All I could think about was that we were finally going to meet.

I gently pulled on the reigns of the horses to bring them to a halt. Then I saw him. There he stood, in front of me. My heartbeat slowed and I felt an aura of peace settle over me.

He stood there, surrounded by his men, each one of them vying for his attention with a witty story or clever joke. Just then his eyes turned and met mine. I knew I should drop by gaze, but I could not look away. Like a deer, I stood there without moving, in front of him and all of his men, until one by one they all turned to look at what their master was staring at. I hoped that he might recognize me. Perhaps he remembered me from before, when I joined the small group of local families that accompanied the hunt, following just behind the aristocracy. With all the charm I could muster, I lowered my head and bowed to him. But when I looked up, I realized there was no warmth in his eyes; there was no softness in the way he was looking at me.

One of the men approached me on foot. His boots were covered in fresh mud, and a smug smile rested across his confident face.

"Our country neighbor, what a pleasant surprise," he said, "Madame d'Etioles, is it?"

I was shocked that he knew me by name. It only took a moment for me to realize this was the Duc de Richelieu. "Good day to you, monsieur," I said with as much warmth and dignity as I possibly could to the chief supporter of Madame de Châteauroux. "I hope you've enjoyed the hunt."

"We most certainly have, thank you. The day has been a great success. It is indeed a pleasure to see you, again. However, his Majesty, the King desires today to be a private ride, and only the nobility will have the privilege of his company. You'll notice that none of the local families have joined the hunt today, not even the men. I bid you good day, Madame," he coolly announced.

It was immediately obvious what he was referring to. By rule, only the families that have been ennobled since the 1400's may have the permission to ride in the King's hunt. Richelieu was very brazenly reminding me of my low birth, that I was not of noble blood and was not welcome in the King's presence. The duke dropped his head ever so slightly, making it clear that he could not be bothered to show too great a respect to someone he felt to be born beneath him, and turning on his heel, returned to the King's side.

And just like that, I had been dismissed. Foolish thing that I was, to think that the King would notice me, that a pretty dress and an impressive entry, an independent, unaccompanied young woman, could gain his attention. How could I have expected that all he would need was to see me, and the attraction between us would suddenly become palpable? How could I have fantasized about something so irrational as a king that would look at a commoner and love her simply as a woman, and a commoner to look at a king and love him for the man that he is and not for the crown on his head? This was not a fairy tale and I was not a princess.

To return home now was out of the question. The moment I set foot in the house, I knew my mother would ask, and the answer would be written on my face. I rode the carriage to the little pond where Alexandrine and I would feed the ducks, and sat by myself for hours. I couldn't bare the company of others. I couldn't bare the questions that were sure to be asked. Everyone would realize that I had been wrong this entire time - that my education and upbringing, all the effort put into preparing me to "reign over the heart of the King," to attain the skills necessary to entertain him, to be deserving of being called 'accomplished,' and be worthy of his love – it was worthless. It had all been a waste.

Now I was to face what I feared the most: I would never know great love. My heart was *not* destined for the King, Madame Lebon lied. It was a foolish idea to begin with. His cold reception of me, ordering Richelieu to send me away, it was clear that I was not and could never be part of that world.

"Now, what am I left with, but a marriage based on friendship that I must settle into," I thought to myself. At most, I could hope that our friendship might evolve into a sort of love and unity, and my great efforts would reach no higher than the establishment of a popular salon. But I wouldn't have the King. I wouldn't have love.

Hours passed. I sat alone, waiting for my favorite time of the day. Just before dusk, the sun would shine golden rays of light onto all that it touched, making the color of the pond an exquisite sparkling azure and the green of the leaves and the hills seem almost mystical. The beauty of this time of the day, with a sky filled with pastel shades of oranges and yellows and pinks, was that there was a sense of mortality to it, lasting perhaps a quarter of an hour until it vanished into a muted, aged blue. Then came darkness. The evening would be arriving soon enough and I must return home.

Quietly I slipped into my bedroom without notice or interruption. My handmaiden was dismissed, and now I struggled to undress by myself. All of these little details and buttons made it impossible for me to remove the gown. Frustrated, I collapsed in a chair, and cried. The tears dropped from my cheeks onto the delicate blue silk fabric. I looked at the gown, my beautiful gown that was sure to catch the eye of the King. I never wanted to see this gown again. Refusing to ring for help, I had no choice but to sleep in the dress I rode out in.

The following morning, I forced myself out of bed after another restless sleep. Dressed, perfumed and powdered, I went down to spend the day in the company of my family. I smiled and listened, trying my best to seem like nothing had happened. But I couldn't deny that I felt different. I felt purposeless.

The servant, dressed in his perfectly tailored and elegantly embroidered uniform, marched into the room looking directly ahead, and upon reaching the center, pivoted to face Monsieur Tournehem and me, who kept me company while my husband was absent on business for the next few months.

"Madame de Brancas," he announced, his gaze directly above my head, then bowed and exited.

No sooner did she walk into the room, than I bounded up to embrace her.

"My dearest, how long it has been since I have seen you, and you look so well," she emphasized.

"Well, I am much better now that I am in your company." She was the one friend I had that brought such joy and life out of me, of whose company I felt most myself in.

After tea with Monsieur Tournehem, he excused himself and I had the pleasure of a private moment in her company, when I could finally share with her what had transpired in the Forest of Sénart. She stared at me with a look of horror on her face, and suddenly burst out laughing.

"How can you find humor in this, when I, myself and horrified and have never felt so lost."

"My dear Jeanne, I laugh because you are so wrong. You have spent the day believing that all is undone, and instead you are saved," and she handed me a letter.

The weight of the paper and the sophistication of the calligraphy hinted at the importance of what information might be contained within the envelope. I couldn't be bothered with retrieving a letter opener, and, as delicately as I could, opened the envelope, reading its contents in silence. Madame de Brancas sat patiently, watching for my reaction, a soft smile spreading across her freshly rouged lips.

"Apparently, your presence in the forest had *not* gone unnoticed," she stated with a sense of triumph in her voice. "It is an invitation to a masked ball in Paris that the King himself will be attending. He has expressed great interest in your presence. In his attempts for his actions to go unobserved by the rest of Court, he will be departing Versailles after the official *couché*, I would imagine, and will of course wear some type of disguise for the event. Once his company at the soiree is noticed, he will be swarmed. It is up to you to steal as much time with him as you can before it is known that the King is present, and leave the greatest impression on him as possible. I need not remind you how greatly the King appreciates discretion, so neither you nor I will mention this to a soul."

CHAPTER X

The year of 1745 had just begun, and I knew that this would be the most important year of my life. Monsieur Tournehem, my mother and I walked through the garden of our estate. Little Fan-Fan, our Alexandrine, scurried ahead in her sweet ivory lace dress with pink satin ribbons. I was so thrilled to share with them the information that Madame de Brancas had told me. I knew both mother and *mon oncle* would be discreet with this sensitive information, and I couldn't resist including them. After all, it with these two who believed in my destiny as much as I did, and it would have been criminal to withhold this experience from them. I expected to receive a million suggestions of what to say and how to act. Instead, they listened patiently to all my thoughts on what I should wear and how we should fix my hair. My mother looked at me with her warm and tender eyes, and gave to me the only advice I ever needed: to be myself. With these two words, she reminded me that the King had endured his share of women who were only interested in him for reasons of power and influence, and that my strength came from loving him for who he is. "Ask nothing of him but his heart, and you will be satisfied," she said.

The morning of the ball, I ordered the curtains closed until noon. I knew very well that tonight I must preserve my energy far past midnight. Once the late afternoon arrived, my handmaiden let the last of the sunlight enter my chamber and lull me awake, while she quietly prepared a bath of milk and rose water for me. My face was powdered with exceptional precision, and the hue of my cheeks and lips highlighted with the rosy pink that made me look my most vibrant and youthful. I carefully chose a regal sapphire blue gown to compliment the bluish grey of my eyes. As a final touch, my handmaiden closed the clasp of my bracelet with the face of Louis XV carved upon the stone on my wrist.

Madame de Brancas had chosen her finest carriage for us to arrive at the ball in. Her gown, though entirely exquisite, was of inferior elegance to my own, and I knew that she had done this purposely, so that I might stand out above the rest tonight.

When we arrived, I couldn't help but be shocked at how overwhelmingly full the soiree had become, and I doubted very much that the King would ever be able to find us in this swarm of gowns and men with swords attached to their hips and servants offering champagne. Madame de Brancas handed the maitre 'd the invitation, and he personally escorted us to a more private alcove, as if he had been expecting our arrival.

Just before the clock struck midnight, I saw two masked men approaching, and I know it was him. I felt my heart shuttering with anticipation and nervousness while I stood there, quite breathless. Noticing Madame de Brancas perform a deep and respectful bow, I followed her example and attempted to do the same.

"You must be that accomplished rider of her own phaeton," one of the men announced, and I instinctively knew this is not the voice of the King, but of his close companion, the Duc d'Ayen. He caught my cheeks blushing at their recollection of perhaps the most embarrassing moment of my life, when I was shunned away from the aristocratic party. "You were a beautiful sight to lay eyes on, Madame, and it was a pity that we had not shared your company that day," he continued. And just like that, my nerves disappeared. I remembered that it was the King who requested my presence at the fête, and I was very much in welcome company. "His Majesty, the King and I are so glad you both were able to join us tonight, however, with such a crowd as this, I doubt very much we will ever be able to find a means of retrieving a glass of champagne. Madame de Brancas, would you be so kind as to accompany me," he said before taking her hand in his and disappearing into the crowd. It was an obvious move to allow the King and I to speak privately.

I had no idea what I should say, and I wasn't quite sure how to act. It seemed obvious that we were all daring to stray from court etiquette, and even more obvious that I shouldn't hold my breath for the King to initiate the topic of conversation.

"I hope your Majesty enjoyed a lovely hunt that day in the forest," I said, choosing the only topic I could think of.

"Very much, thank you. I have heard from a relative of yours, Sieur Binet, that there are few more familiar with that forest than yourself."

I smiled at the thought of him talking about me when I wasn't around. "I do pride myself of a thorough knowledge of Sénart, though that has greatly to do with the fact that it is your Majesty's favorite hunting grounds," I said, knowing quite well that hunting was one of the King's favorite topics, and the easiest way to engage in conversation with him.

Savoring the luxury of our private conversation with the most handsome man in France, I found myself enchanted with every aspect of him. Pretending that I couldn't hear him above the crowd, I dipped my head closer, but it was only to eliminate all distractions and more clearly hear the resonating depth of his voice, to breathe him in.

His dress was decidedly understated this evening. I noticed his ordinary black jacket, white shirt peaking through, and ruffled tie wrapped perfectly around the sturdy thickness of his neck, and it became clear that he had made every effort to go unnoticed. His face had been, of course, cleanly shaven that morning and now at this hour, the hint of shadow of fresh facial hair was beginning to show, perfectly framing the warmth I felt in the gaze of his trustworthy brown eyes.

The conversation turned to mutual friends, one of which was my beloved Voltaire. Many were of the opinion that Voltaire was entirely against the Church and State, mainly because of a number of pamphlets Voltaire had published recently that had gained him even more notoriety. He was glorified in Paris and shunned by the Church for questioning the privileges that the King generously allowed.

"Voltaire is an exceptional intellect and an acknowledged visionary," I said. "Despite what ideas his persona may evoke, I promise *Son Excellence* that, throughout his visits to my salon, our conversations only provoked thought and never revolution. I am sure you could find no greater patriot than Voltaire."

"We are in great need of men with minds that match their hearts," the King conceded. "It would be a pleasure to meet him." He glanced to his left, and I could tell he was thinking. Instinctually I held my breath, wondering what ideas his beautiful mind was wandering to. "There will be a masked ball at Versailles in two weeks time, the eighth of February. Will you do me the honor of joining me?"

"You have no idea how greatly I desire to," I answered, reaching to touch his hand for the first time. An unabashed smile spread across my face. I could not pretend to be coy when my heart was singing.

The following weeks were like a fairytale. Each day I slept until noon and bathed in warm milk, followed by a mask of egg yoke and honey for an hour, to ensure that my skin looked impeccable for the ball. This was to become a regular routine to keep up my energy and appearance. It was imperative that I prepare myself for what was to come.

Throughout the month, the King had organized several festivities to celebrate the marriage of his son, the Dauphin, with Maria Teresa Rafaela, the Infanta of Spain. Politically, these ceremonies and events were essential. After years of discontent that resulted from the King breaking off the engagement to the Infanta's older sister nearly twenty years ago, France and Spain had come to an arrangement that the Infanta of Spain was now to be the bride to his son, in hopes that their ties would be repaired.

When the evening of the eighth arrived, I spent the entire night at the King's side. Our masked faces disguising well the woman who wouldn't be parted from the arms of his Majesty, but his Court had little doubt as to the identity of the man at my side. The ball spread throughout the royal apartments, and we danced uninterrupted for hours. The way that he held me to him, I sensed that the man who was known to be bashful around unfamiliar faces was growing more and more comfortable with me in his arms.

Nearly each night that month, the King, romantic being that he was, would dutifully fulfill the ceremony of going to bed, the *couché*, before sneaking out to meet me privately. Great measures were taken to protect our privacy, but it was all in vain. The Court of Versailles was like a well-connected organism, especially with gossip of the King's interest in a new woman. As the weeks of February went on and our evenings together continued from the ball at Versailles to a masquerade in the town, it was noted by many that the King was loyally by one, and only one woman's side. Little by little, the veil of privacy and secrecy that guarded his words came tumbling down, and I felt his heart welcoming me in.

The night before the wedding of the Dauphin and the Infanta of Spain we enjoyed a ball at the Hôtel de Ville in Paris. The evening could not be more enchanting, yet I could tell that his thoughts were elsewhere. Though I dared not ask what was distracting him, I wondered if he was thinking of his son's ball that was to be celebrated the next day. Did he wish to celebrate the day with Madame de Châteauroux? I understood that it was impossible for me to attend the ceremony. I was not of the nobility.

Although we had spent much time together, and although I knew that I was entirely in love with him, I doubted very much that his heart was as sure of itself as mine. He was deeply in love with his former mistress, and he had only just met me. "If she were still alive," I thought to myself, "she would be here by his side, and unlike me, she would be able to go to the wedding and share in this momentous occasion in the King's life."

The day of the wedding, I heard not a word from the King. He was busy, of course, and I couldn't be upset that his time was occupied with the celebration of his firstborn son's wedding.

"Have patience," the wise Madame de Brancas reminded me, "his duties are many, particularly on such a monumental occasion. But don't give in to fear; he has not forgotten you." And she was right. A note arrived before evening that the day after the wedding there would be a private event by invitation only at the Large Stables in Versailles, and I was to come.

"Tell me of the ceremony. I do so love weddings," I begged the King, hoping to not sound upset at being unable to attend the event.

"My dear, I admit that I haven't seen Versailles so glorious in all my life. The entire chateau was illuminated. Cardinal Rohan performed the marriage, and the bride had no equal in beauty or grace. I do believe I have made a perfect match for my son, the Dauphin," he said with the content pride of a father who has managed the difficult task of creating a happy pair. "They are both quite shy, but they will grow accustomed to one another over time, I am sure of it," he went on, with a bit of concern in his voice, and I knew he was thinking about the gossip surrounding the Dauphin and his bride. The newlyweds had not consummated their marriage on their wedding night. Knowing the Court as he did, I understood that this would be an embarrassment for the young bride, and a concern for the King, who desired very much to see little heirs produced for France.

"And how was the performance? I believe the words were by none other than my Voltaire," I inquired, changing the subject to something more lighthearted, and with less political and personal relevance.

"Ah, the *Princesse de Navarre*. I was quite happy with the play, and both Voltaire and Rameau did well to produce this work for the wedding," he conceded, choosing his words carefully.

"You are too kind, Sire." I laughed. "The courtiers, so I have heard, are not so forgiving in their judgment."

"They never are, yet I am certain that this was just the first of many performances and plays to come. Voltaire's star is on the rise. Now tell me, Madame d'Etioles, how do you find your accommodations?" There was a mixture of flirtation and curiosity to see my reaction to the place he had chosen for me.

I couldn't help but laugh out loud, for I knew very well how difficult it was to ensure a room was available during this time, and that it was him whom had been behind the arrangements. "Why, thank you for asking. In fact, just a few days prior, the President Henault had inquired into the same subject when he discovered that I will be attending the ball tomorrow night."

"And how did you answer him?"

"That my cousin, Sieur Binet, was very kind to look into it for me."

The King let out a hearty laugh. "Well done, you are already turning into a courtier," he joked. This courtship could be a difficult thing to maneuver through, particularly in our attempts to shield our affections from the public eye. Privacy was of utmost interest to me. I wanted the King to discover his true feelings for me before his Court found out of the affair and gave their opinion. I wanted him to discover his feelings for me before they were disrupted or imposed upon by others.

And yet, I took great comfort in one very telling act. I found myself comfortably placed in a small bedroom with two windows and a room to receive company. But the importance of the room was not in the comfort, but that the King had specifically chosen to place me in the former apartment of Madame de Mailly.

CHAPTER XI

The coaches, filled with the expectations of excited guests from the city, rolled along in well-formed rows of two by two leading down the torch lit Avenue de Paris. The capital's most beautifully dressed women all arrived, and I knew just as well as the next that each one of these women who believed the King was unattached had planned that tonight would be their chance to try their hand at his royal heart. Unlike last evening, tonight's masked ball was entirely open to the public, and everyone showed up. I saw the men fiddling with invitations and, for those that did not have their own sword strapped to their hip, they hurried to rent a sword, an absolutely necessary accessory, from the concierge. But the crowd was enormous, and it would be only a matter of time before any attempt to regulate entry was given up.

I exited my carriage at the southern wing of the palace, and felt the warmth of the fire from the candles and torches lining the outside. Inside, I found people sampling the buffet, listening to the musicians, and rushing like waves from one room to the next. Unabashedly, the crowd even made their way into the Queen's rooms, and the courtiers voiced their shock at the lack of etiquette of the Parisians. Everyone was dressed in their finest wardrobe, but there was a distinct separation between the way that the courtier dressed. Their attire was impeccable and bold, as if they were using their dress to distinguish their superior rank over the bourgeois.

Search though I might, the King was nowhere to be found. Calmly, I passed from one room to the next, hoping that if I could not see the King, that he would find me. In all corners I could hear whispers and gossip of whom the King was with, that he was most probably stealing a moment alone with her at this very moment. I couldn't help but feel that sting of fear and jealousy, for the King and I had only just recently been spending time together, and there was a sea of women more beautiful and better born than I to catch his attention.

Her Majesty the Queen entered unmasked, followed by her son and his new bride. The Queen was dressed gloriously, with pearls and diamonds sewn into her gown, and the newlyweds were very sweetly dressed as a gardener and his flower-seller. There was a great expectation in the air that the King would follow behind, but he was nowhere in sight.

Finally, the doors to the King's apartment opened, and all eyes turned to see a line of eight identical yew trees that looked as if they had plucked their roots from the well-manicured gardens of Versailles and were now proceeding forward into the crowd. It seemed only a matter of moments before they began pairing off with beautifully gowned women. I noticed the lovely Présidente Portail and one of the eight trees nestle into a dark solitary corner, and knew immediately from her flirtatious body language that she thought she was speaking with the King.

Looking at her, I felt pity for the King, who had so many attempts by women who wished to seduce him for his title and the power that being his mistress would yield. I wondered if he were used to it by now, and if he knew that I was not like the others. I wanted none of that; I knew very well that ambition would only lead to emptiness. I wanted love. I wanted to be beckoned by the call of love and to respond to it with my entire being. I wanted to wake, enfolded in the arms of my lover and to yield to him completely.

"Nothing short of a goddess," he whispered from behind me, "you must know me well, to have chosen to rule over the hunt," gesturing to my choice of dressing as the Greek goddess Diana.

"It seemed only fair that I am to rule over the hunt, your Majesty, for it is you that rules my heart." It wasn't the nature of other women to speak as boldly as I did to his Majesty. The month was coming to an end and I did not know how much longer I had the King's attention. But I would not fail to expose just how strongly my heart beat for him. I reached out and removed his headdress to see the warmth of his smiling eyes, and he removed my mask as well. I wanted so badly for this man, a man who could not remember the love of a mother he had lost at such a tender age, to know the harmony of a reciprocating love from a selfless heart. I wanted him to feel secure in the sincerity and purity of my feelings for him.

"They are saying that the 'handkerchief has been thrown,'" announced Madame d'Estrade, as she proudly strode into my little apartments. "It is being said that this is more than a passing dalliance with a simple bourgeois."

"Is that so," I reached out to embrace her, and felt the weakness in my body from the simple act of standing. After so many late nights, I was exhausted. "And pray tell, who is spreading such gossip?"

"The Duc de Luynes, of course. Why, just last week he was saying that the King stayed in bed until five in the afternoon after returning that morning from a ball at Hôtel de Ville in Paris where he had spent the entire night with you."

I smiled as I considered how thoughtful the King was that evening. People came pouring into the Hôtel de Ville, with such a crowd that I was entirely overwhelmed. I must have looked as frightened as I was disheveled, for when the King found me, he promptly covered me in his black cloak and brought me back to the Hôtel de Gesvres.

"Don't pay any attention to that old dud, Jeanne-Antoinette. He was a fool to say that you are nothing but a distraction for the King, and that you would never be more than a flirtation. The Duc de Luynes certainly changed his tune when he heard that you were at the theatre, and now I hear you are in with the King's inner circle, at his *petit cabinets*. Shame on you for failing to mention that, even to me, your greatest confidant," she admonished.

"I am sorry, my friend. These past few months have been a whirlwind, and I hardly find time in the day to rest before I must prepare for another evening, but I would hate for you to feel neglected."

"Well, I suppose that I do feel neglected," she said, annoyed with me. "I've left Paris for you and am here in Versailles among all of these judgmental people, and now I find myself quite abandoned."

"Now, don't say such things. You must come tomorrow evening. I will speak with the King and let him know that you are my guest.

It will just be a small group of us, just the Duc de Richelieu, the Duc d'Ayens, and perhaps the Duc de Boufflers and de Luxembourg will be there as well. But it would be a delight to have the comfort of you with me as I grow more acquainted with his closest friends."

The following day, I spoke with Madame de Brancas of my conversation with Madame d'Estrades.

"Jeanne-Antoinette, you were not wise in inviting that woman to join the King. He will no doubt enjoy her company. Madame d'Estrades is no beauty, you have no threat there. But the King loves little stories of gossip, and few are more willing to talk about other's affairs than her. But be warned, Madame d'Estrades is not a woman to be trusted. Please do not be insulted when I tell you that I find her to be manipulative and self-serving, and I myself have heard her plant seeds of doubt about the love of the King into your head."

"Your concern touches my heart, but I assure you that Madame d'Estrades has my best interest in mind."

"You were her entry into Court, and she will use you as long as you are of use," she stated matter-of-factly.

"I understand, and thank you. But I have so few friends here, I cannot afford to alienate myself from her."

"You are correct, my dear. You can be certain that there are but a few you will be able to truly consider friends at Court. I cannot even pass through a corridor in the palace without hearing your name mentioned. They're all talking of catching a glimpse of you passing in and out of Versailles, and the King insisting to eat alone, meanwhile they all suspect you are in his company. The King's affections for you have not gone unnoticed, particularly now that you are spending more time with his closest friends. But just because he is welcoming you into his innermost world, his innermost world will not be welcoming of you. At present, you are looked at as nothing more than a passing fling and a fun subject of gossip, but soon they will look at you as an intruder."

"An intruder? I can't imagine anyone looking at me as a threat."

"But in their minds, you are just that: a threat, for the King is entirely in love with you, and if you are to become his mistress, many will look at it as polluting the superiority of court tradition with the mediocrity of the middle class, and taking the position that a courtier has been born and bred for."

"Thank you, my friend. I can always count on you to speak the truth instead of telling me what I want to hear. The King and I have grown so close throughout the last few months, I hardly spend a night away from him. But as much as he opens his heart to me and as well as I understand him, I sense the existence of a profound barrier that distances how close he will let me into his life. In fact, when it is just the two of us, he is delighted with the funny little nuances of how distinct my Parisian ways are from the ways of the Court, but when we are in public, I sense that he may be embarrassed by it."

"Versailles is an altogether different universe, with its own use of words, mannerisms, and etiquette, and the King values the respect and adoration of his Court and countrymen. If he feels that your ways make you stand out, it is a poor reflection on him. It does not help the matter that there are men like the Duc de Richelieu instilling a sense of embarrassment in him by arguing that loving a commoner brings disgrace to the name of the King, particularly a king who has made every effort to honor the traditions that his grandfather Louis XIV instilled."

"I would rather die than bring dishonor onto my King, but I cannot be parted with him. I could not bare it. I cannot change who I am, just as I cannot change the situation into which I have been born into any more than he," I said, overwhelmed. "It only gets more complicated." I walked over to my desk and unlocked the drawer, removing an envelope. "I am to now choose if I must sacrifice my entire life to be a part of his world where I will be loved by him but despised by all who surround me, or return to the simple and respected life I had before."

Madame de Brancas listened quietly for me to continue, and I handed her the note from my husband.

"Monsieur d'Etioles just recently returned from Provence where he went for business, and Monsieur Tournehem regretted to have to inform him of my relations with the King. My poor husband was so distraught that he couldn't help but write me a letter, imploring me to return to our life and family," I said, as I rubbed my finger where my wedding ring once was. "It breaks my heart that I am the cause of my husband's suffering, and I am beginning to doubt if the sacrifice will be worth it. I couldn't hide this from the King, and felt it only fair to show him the letter. If you could have seen his reaction, his disappointment in me, as if I had done the most improper act by exposing my husband's private thoughts to my lover."

"Naturally he was shocked by your behavior. A courtier would never have acted so indiscreetly. Why did you feel that you must show him such a personal letter?"

"I only meant to be completely open, to hide nothing of myself from him. Only now do I see that the King felt it was disrespectful to my husband to share something so delicate to the man that's taken his place. But I needed to know where I stand with him. The King loves me, but between my place as a bourgeois and the growing list of enemies I am gaining at Court, I wonder if I will ever be anything more than an interest for him. And so, I wanted him to be aware of what this will cost me."

A smile spread widely across her face. "You may be the bravest one of us all, Madame d'Etioles, if not the most clever. For the King prides himself on being a gentleman, and you have now brought it to his attention that a moment has arisen where he can, with decency, safely deposit you back into the welcoming arms of your awaiting husband, *or* that he can instill you properly into the Court, but that the choice must be made."

"I cannot imagine how I will ever be "instilled properly into the Court," as you say. The courtier's behaviors, even their values, are not only entirely different from my own, but border on ridiculous. Why, just the other day I overheard a woman chiding her friend for bowing too low to someone who didn't merit such respect. Such a concern is pure foolishness in my eyes, and yet, is entirely normal in theirs. Am I to forget my instinct and good sense, and instead evolve into a member of this society that lacks all reason and bases such value on to petty issues?"

"This is the culture that the King exists in. He does not have the ability to enter your world of salons with philosophers or financiers, so you must rise to the occasion to enter into his. Besides, haven't I heard that you are one of France's best actresses? Surely, you won't have any trouble learning the rules and acting the part."

"But after such a blunder, the King must view me as vulgar. If you are right, and I have now brought him into a situation where he must choose to keep me by his side or return me, I doubt very much he will choose the former," I feared.

"Nonsense," she interrupted me. "Have you ever heard of a man that did not appreciate a woman delighting in him as you do the King? And the entertainment you bring him is endless. Your humor and affection, this is exactly what he looks forward to escaping to after the Court has spent the entire day fussing over him. There's been no other that delights in him, or performs for him the way you do, singing your little songs and interesting anecdotes of Paris. He values you, and you will only grow to become more indispensable to him with the passing of time. Why, everyone comments on how deeply in love you both are, I am sure that won't change."

"Thank you for your kind words, dear friend, for they indeed give courage. But I must admit that I fear very much for what is to become of our love. The King and Dauphin are preparing to leave for campaign, and I am not to join."

"I am sure this is a result of the Metz affair and how badly it was handled by that wicked Châteauroux woman," Madame de Brancas said, as if she were thinking out loud. "But don't loose heart, if you are to be parted with the King, what better time to grow accustomed to courtly ways. Make use of this time apart. Encourage the King on his journey, and while he is away, you will need a tutor to school you in the practices of his world at Court. And whatever you do, make it seem like this was his idea."

CHAPTER XII

Her advice was sagacious, and the King elected two hand-chosen men to act as my tutors so that I might survive Court and all of its treacherous traps that all the beauties of Versailles would have loved to see me fall in. But the King knew better, and so I was to live for the next four months at Etioles, and be educated by the Abbé de Bernis and the Marquis de Gontaut.

The Abbé de Bernis had made quite a fuss about having to instruct a mere bourgeois, but any reluctance he may have had was swayed by the great honor of being commissioned by the King. Once I met him, it took me only a minute to realize that he was merely feigning resignation for appearance's sake, and was actually quite honored that, of all men the King could have chosen to educate his beloved, the King had selected him. But with his dimpled cheeks, endearing humor and cultured manner, I loved him at once and it was only a matter of time before he was taken with my charms as well. And it didn't hurt that the King had done him the great honor of suggesting his election into the Academie Française.

The Marquis de Gontaut was an entirely unique creature from the Abbé. Unlike Bernis, the Marquis was born into the highest levels of aristocracy yet had no airs about him, and was a very dear friend of the King's. He was, from the very first moment we met, one of the kindest friends I had, and I soon realized that he was a man of great morality and loyalty.

Their mission was set out for them. Within a matter of months, they would have to teach me the customs of Court, and I would have to unlearn my bourgeois habits. But I couldn't allow myself to feel overwhelmed. Instead I had to look at everyday as an opportunity to learn more from these cultivated minds. I was completely ignorant of the customs I was now not only expected to know, but to excel at, and in only a matter of months. The King, I hoped, would only be gone for a short time. My only concern was that, by the time he returned, the Abbé and the Marquis would groom me to the point that I wouldn't embarrass him in front of his Court.

My education began with language. But what I considered the basics proved to be one of the most challenging adjustments I was to make. Versailles had a particular manner of speaking, it was one of the ways they distinguished themselves from the rest as the superior social class. The nuances of Versailles were subtle, but would be immediately recognizable to the courtier. There were words and phrases that I must learn or avoid in order to not expose myself as an outsider of their "*petit pais.*"

Next came lessons of aristocracy. Patiently my two faithful courtiers explained in the greatest detail each of the families at Court and how to esteem them based on their ranking. A courtier of modest birth might receive a shallow curtsey, while a duke would be insulted with nothing less than a reverent curtsey that expressed proper respect of his distinguished rank. In the presence of the royal family, one courtier might enter a room and be expected to stand, while another would receive a stool, and a third would be entitled to a chair. The new manner in which I was to sit and stand, how I was to use my utensils and hold my wine glass were all practiced a hundred times over. Instead of walking as I normally did, I was taught to move as if I were gliding across the floor, like a divine nymph of the French court. And above all, my tutors stressed that a courtier must, without fail, be of good spirits. Versailles did not tolerate sadness, regardless of how one felt. Every gesture, every action I made would either prove that I could fit in, or alienate me as a bourgeois that didn't belong. It was an artificial existence, but if I were to share my life with the King, I had no choice but to adapt.

My mother and father, my brother Abel and Tournehem visited often. My mother was greatly relieved to see how much my health improved in the countryside, where I was able to sleep without interruption and drink in that clean open air. My mother, however relieved as she was at my strength, could not hide her failing health, and nothing broke my heart more than to see her age and know that

I couldn't slow down the passing of time. But she wouldn't hear a thing about it. She would not indulge in sadness, and refused to let me worry myself with her health.

"My life," she promised, "is a sequence of moving from one joy to the next. Our sweet Alexandrine is at the village with a nursemaid nearby where we visit nearly every day, and I am witnessing my daughter experience love and rise in greatness."

Madame d'Estrades, who was also a very good friend of the Abbé de Bernis,' made for very good company. She joined the Marquis and I one afternoon, just as the mail was being delivered.

"Ah, Madame has received not one note today, but two," she teased, picking up the letters that the servant brought in on a silver tray. "The first, another declaration of undying love, I am sure, from his Majesty. The second from… a Monsieur Voltaire?" she said with a sort of shock and admiration. "Well," she pressed, "what did he say?"

"Dear Voltaire," I said, folding the letter back into the envelope. "He wants to come visit and have a word with me in private."

"I am sure he does, the old womanizer."

"Oh, don't call him that. He is one of the greatest men of our time. Who else is as prolific of a writer as he? It comes as no surprise that women flock to him," I replied, defensively.

"I am not saying he is a libertine. I'm only suggesting that you are the most beautiful woman in Paris and soon to be the toast of Versailles. It's only natural that he would want to claim allegiance to you during your ascent," she retorted. "Don't accuse me of labeling him as something he is not. You know that I have the greatest respect for that man, but you must keep in mind who you ally yourself with now," she warned.

"Thank you, dear friend, for your concern. But Voltaire has been a great friend of mine for ages now, as you well know, and I trust he has no ulterior motives."

"Then you trust too easily," interjected the voice of the Marquis de Gontaut, looking from me to Madame d'Estrades. "Everyone you encounter from this moment forward will have motives, and will see you as a tool to support their ambitions. Friend one may very well be, but without ambition one is not."

It did not take me long to find that, having come from a family as distinguished as the Biron's, the Marquis de Gontaut had no need for ambition and was by no means pretentious. Many noblemen used marriage as an exchange of title for wealth, while others felt the need to constantly remind others of how grand they are. Because he had been born into such a respected level of society, he never felt the need to remind anyone of who he was or from where he came. It simply went unsaid. In this way, he stood as a stark contract to others.

When I reflected on what the marquis was trying to imply, it was not all aimed at Voltaire. Instead the marquis was suggesting that I must be aware that, as I was entering into a role of influence at Court, some might try to take advantage of their relationship with me, while others would require my safeguarding, and I must use discernment.

I had the pleasure of receiving Voltaire during the month of May. I was partially nervous for his visit. He had the tendency, as great men often do, of entering into those dark recesses of his mind that at times made him appear sour or bitter. But it turned out that I had nothing to be concerned about. During his entire stay, he was charming and content.

"Remind me, *ma charmante amie*," he said, as we walked through the gardens, "how did Babet *le bouquetiere* find his way into your household?" Voltaire began one afternoon once we found a moment to speak in private.

"Where in the world did you come up with this nickname for the Abbé de Bernis?"

"Oh, don't scold me. Though I would be delighted to have come up with the name myself, he is very well-known in Paris society by this name. Besides, you must admit, the name is nothing, if not fitting, considering his poetry."

"The Abbé does me great honor with the time he has dedicated to my instruction of courtly ways. I am very much in his debt," I said, playfully pitching the inside of his arm. "But you are just in your assessment of his poetry."

"Anyway, Jeanne-Antoinette. You are the first to know my great respect for the man. He is good company, and always has one anecdote or another to entertain. I am only surprised that he has been honored with the privilege of so much time in your company."

"Oh, I know you too well after all these years, *mon philospophe*. You must know, after all the time you and I have spent together, I can see right through you."

"Indeed, I was hoping as much. I expected that you would see the great jealousy I have of these two gentlemen who have the honor of your time, while your dear Voltaire is much forgotten in the drab of the city and the life you once lived," he lovingly lectured.

"Hush," I said. "You know only too well how deep my adoration is for you, and how highly I speak your praises to the King."

"Madame," he said, his voice growing serious, "that is precisely what I was hoping to hear. You must know how greatly your friends from Paris admire you and send you warm thoughts as you venture onto this exciting chapter in your life. We very much expect that you will come to rule all the ladies of Versailles. We only hope you will remember the friendship of your youth. We will have need of your protection."

"My protection?" I asked. "Protection from what, or whom?"

Voltaire inhaled deeply, as he considered how to phrase what he wanted to say.

Before he could say another word, I interjected. "*Mon ami*, please speak not with your mind, but with your heart."

He slowed his pace of walking and turned to me. "Jeanne-Antoinette, you have sat with us through our discussions in your salon, you know our principles. I need not remind you that our beliefs and debates are to ensure the progress of the French people."

"Yes, of course I do. And the King knows very well that your convictions are founded on a depth and purity of patriotism."

"But our beliefs are very distinct from those of the Jesuits, who at every chance try to slander us or paint our dialogue as against God and King. They act as if our beliefs are heretical, and it is concerning to think whose ear at Court they are bending." His emotions were getting the better of him, and he paused to regain his composure. "The world is evolving, yet there is always great danger in encouraging thoughts that are not in agreement with the powerful few. All I ask is that you speak on our behalf to his Majesty, that he realizes how entirely devoted we are to the preservation of the future of France."

"You honor me too greatly. Surely I will do absolutely everything in my power to protect and support you, but whatever influence you think I have over the King is misguided thought. I love a powerful man, but there is no authority in the sentiment."

"Have you forgotten your predecessors, the great Montespan, or the Marquise de Maintenon? Did they not have the weight to sway their beloved's judgment to and fro? Your ability to influence the King will be of equal authority. Remember this conversation, may it be held as truth, that the King will honor you by placing you in a position of power, and when that moment comes, you will consider and protect your friends."

Voltaire did us the honor of visiting us on different occasions throughout that summer. I knew very well that I was in the company of a visionary, and took advantage of our time together to learn. But my time with him also reminded me of the freedom I exercised in my salon. There, I was exposed to a mixture of brilliance of mind and personality. It was clear that I would not have that same pleasure of diversity and freedom at Versailles, where there was a uniformity of speech and mannerisms that were considered *en vogue*.

Voltaire entertained us all with updates on the events of bustling Paris, and informed us of the literature that was gaining attention in the city. There were many geopolitical events developing abroad, in England and her developing colony of America, and Voltaire was very concerned about how this would influence the rest of the world.

That word, 'influence,' stuck out to me. The tiny island of England was shaping the future of this massive territory of America. Since the mid 1500's, France had her influence in the Americas as well, and was recognized as having much better relations with the indigenous tribes than England. While Spain and England overpowered or neglected the Indians, the French offered them equality and French citizenship upon conversion to Catholicism. But it seemed that the French influence in the Americas couldn't compete with that of the English, whose population continued to multiply. Through colonization, England had taken the New World under her authority, promising modernization, and the future of that foreign land lay subject to the actions of its 'mother country.'

Upon voicing these thoughts to Voltaire, he simply said, "if England can develop America into to a proper country with government, economy, and propriety, how much more can you, young Jeanne-Antoinette, bring progress to that old Court and their outdated norms established nearly a century ago."

"I can confidently say that I doubt very much to have such an impact at a court that won't even receive me."

"We cannot be so short-sighted, my dear. It is only a matter of time before you will not only be received, you will be the center of attention. And when that time comes, your sense of style, your behaviors and opinions, it will all be noted, discussed, and often mimicked. I have already seen you accomplish such feats at the salons of Paris, now onward and upward you go to Versailles," he announced with cheeky authority in his tone. "For, if the King had not intended for you to impact his Court, he would not have invested so greatly in you as to have chosen these two men to educate you in the ways of Versailles and all its intricate details. Now, it is up to you as to how you will use such influence."

CHAPTER XIII

"Wake up!" cried my handmaiden, her voice screeching. She unceremoniously pulled the covers off of me and hurried to find my robe in the darkness. "There's been an attack!"

I fumbled for my lamp, and the two of us hurried down the steps of the staircase to find the entire household huddled together in the living room. No one noticed us enter the room; all eyes were on the black smoke reaching to the heavens. Each of them stood silently, waiting to hear a cannon explode, screams, anything that would indicate what had happened, and if we were truly under attack.

"It is nothing more than an accident, some minor explosion," came the calm frankness of the Marquis de Gontaut. "Off to bed, ladies, there is nothing to be alarmed about," he said, settling down onto the feather filled chair near the window.

"I'll stay awake with you," I said. "I won't be able to sleep well after this anyway."

"No, no. I'll be going to sleep in a moment as well, and you need your rest, Madame. Do get some rest, it is so important for your health."

In my letter to the King the next day, hoping to not cause him unnecessary fear for my life or distract him from his focus on the war, I only briefly mentioned the fire. I explained that we discovered it had been an explosion from a powder magazine not far from us, in the neighboring town of Corbeil, and reassured him that the matter was nothing to be concerned about.

By the evening of the following day, I grew nervous. It was the first day that I did not receive a letter from the King. He consistently wrote me everyday since our separation. Since May, he had sent nearly eighty letters to Pâris de Montmartel who would then send them onward to me. It was unlike him to not write, and I couldn't help but feel uneasy.

Days passed and my anxiety grew. What could possibly be impeding these letters? His feelings could not be so fleeting, I was sure of it. The King loved me. And I couldn't bare to imagine any other reason for his not writing.

Finally, after what felt like an eternity of silence, Pâris de Montmartel personally arrived from Brunoy with my letter.

"My goodness," I said, meeting him outside by the carriage, "this letter took much longer than expected."

"It must contain something special," he answered, handing me the letter.

"It's addressed differently, to *à Madame la Marquise de Pompadour, à Etioles*. What's this?" I said aloud, breaking the crimson seal stamped with the King's ring and removing the contents. Enclosed I found the deeds to an estate of Pompadour, along with a marquisate that had previously been expired, and a coat of arms of three white castles set against a blue background.

Holding the thick, luxurious paper in my hands, I felt a sense of elation and peace settle into my heart. 'A marquise,' I pondered on the word, the elegant sound of the title my beloved King had bestowed upon me. But the satisfaction I felt was not that I was no longer a commoner; my position mattered so very little to me. The true significance in this title was for one reason. He had made his decision; the King had chosen me. No longer would I be loved at arms distance. From this moment on, I would be part of his life.

The King and his son, Monsieur Le Dauphin, returned from their battle against the British at Fontenoy, victorious and celebrated by all France. Most important to me, he returned uninjured. All of Paris was delighted at his safe return and glorious triumph against France's hated enemy. The jubilant streets were filled with singing and parties at the Hôtel de Ville to celebrate their royal return, and the city feverishly ate up Voltaire's poem of the heroic battle, which he wisely dedicated to his Majesty. The royal family and their court returned to their home in Versailles in early September, and I to my new apartment, where the King and I privately supped in my quarters.

"More and more, I feel like these short moments I have alone with you is the only escape I am allowed," he told me one night while

I rested in his arms, leaning against his chest and silently looking at that crackling fireplace. He picked up the original copy of the poem that Voltaire had gifted me with, and carefully leafed through it. "It seems all anyone will speak about is the war, the glorious war," a melancholy sigh escaping his perfectly formed lips.

"Your nation is proud of you, of your leadership, fighting right alongside your men," I encouraged.

"There is hardly any glory to war. I saw men being blown apart, lives lost, brave men who will never again return to the arms of their lovely sweethearts, the way I am able to return to you. Once the battle was over," he went on, "I led my son around the grounds. He needed to see with his own eyes the costs of war, that it must be avoided."

There were no words I could say that would remove the horror of what he had seen. His heart was troubled, and I couldn't fix it. I sat up and held his head close to my heart, stroking his thick dark hair and humming soothingly.

"You have no idea how much your presence eases my mind. Jeanne-Antoinette, I need you here more than you know. I can't imagine returning to Court without you."

"I will be right here, whenever you need me," I promised with all my heart.

"Right here is not close enough. I have made arrangements," he stated. "You are to be presented at Court."

CHAPTER XIV

Late that evening, the carriage came to a halt near a small side door of the palace, where a single servant was waiting.

"I am so relieved you are here with me," I said to Madame d'Estrades. "I couldn't bear doing this on my own."

"Of course you couldn't, dear. The Court would eat you whole if you were on your own. Besides, it makes sense that I join you. You will need a familiar face, and I am of the nobility." I smiled to myself at my friend's funny way of complimenting herself. She always stressed the title of nobility she gained through her marriage to her belated husband, but she, herself was born a bourgeois, just like me.

"Still, it's overwhelming. Such a privilege is deserving of those that have generations of noble blood."

She could see that I was growing anxious. "Yes, but you are no longer simply Madame d'Etioles. You are the Marquise de Pompadour. You have been ennobled, so act the part."

I toyed with my gloves nervously, and took a deep breath to calm myself before the servant opened the door. I understood that it would be impossible for the King to be the one to greet me. Protocol forbade it, and more importantly, I knew it wasn't in his nature to make a grand entrance of his new official mistress. He preferred discretion, and establishing a Parisian bourgeois as his official *maîtresse* would already cause enough undue attention.

Madame d'Estrades and I were led through a side door of the palace and up a flight of stairs, until a servant led her to her private chamber, and me to mine. The King was there, waiting for me. The servant bowed and exited, understanding that we desired privacy.

"Are you happy?" he asked.

"More than you know."

"Your hands are shaking, you must be freezing."

I didn't want to admit that really, I was just so nervous.

"Forgive me, but I feel that I have been waiting for this moment my entire life. I have loved you always. I dreamed of being near you, never having to be separated from you. But I never thought I would be presented at Court," I said. The King stared at me unmoving. I blushed at my own over-exposure of my feelings, and felt ashamed at myself for such lack of composure, again proving that I was not a native of his Court. "I am sorry, I imagine that's not the way other women at Versailles behave."

"No, it's not, and that's precisely why I find you so refreshing. Of anyone I've ever met, you make me feel truly loved." Taking my hand, he led me to a door, inside which sat a swing.

"Get in, there's something I want to show you."

I sat in the chair, and he took the chord and lowered me down to another room. Moments later, he met me down there.

"This is my refuge, one of my favorite places in the world, the *petits cabinets*."

The room was warm, comfortable. I wandered to the different rooms, and realized that this was where he came to escape. Unlike the rest of Versailles, the rooms had an air of modernity and comfort.

"It often gets cold in these rooms, so I lit the fire for us. Would you like some coffee?" he asked. I shook my head, surprised that the King of France was performing tasks traditionally assigned to a servant. "Here, look at this. This is my distillery, and over there is my own little kitchen, I am told I make exceptional pastries."

"And what is this?" I asked, walking over to what looked like a workman's station.

"Ah, you've discovered one of my favorite pastimes. This is where I do my wood working," he said, showing me a collection of objects he had crafted.

"What are your other favorite pastimes?" I asked, gently flirting with him.

"I have but two, hunting and you." He pulled me close, wrapping his arms around my waist. His lips gently caressed my neck, then my cheek, the corner of my mouth, and finally my lips.

The next day, Madame d'Estrades was presented at Court. She entered my rooms, jubilant with self-satisfaction.

"You must rehearse how to curtsy," she lectured. "It's very important that you practice, and I will help you to perfect it. But make sure you do practice," she stressed, "or else you will look like a bafoon and the Court will all laugh."

"I promise to practice, but in the mean time, we will be supping this evening privately with His Majesty and a select few of his friends."

"Excellent, we are now part of his inner circle," she boasted.

"No," I corrected, "we are getting to know his inner circle, and I hope very much to make a good impression."

"Anyway, the King succeeded in finding someone to present you."

"Was it difficult?"

"For him to find someone to present his mistress? Of course," she laughed. "I overheard that the King has secured the Princesse de Conti to perform the task. He finally won the old bag over. She was prepared to refuse him, until he suggested that he would pay off her gambling debts. Her son is horrified, but how could she refuse?"

Madame d'Estrades' behavior made me nervous. She had an air of superiority to her, and I didn't like it. I had been warned that the courtiers would never look at me as their equal, but I didn't want pretentious behavior to make me enemies. But I reassured myself that her reaction was a natural response of the great honor of being presented at Court, and soon she would settle into life as a courtier.

"You will be presented on the 16th," the Marquis de Gontaut announced.

"That is tomorrow."

"Yes, we have but a little time to prepare, Jeanne Antoinette. The ceremony will take place at 6pm, and we have much to practice."

"Madame d'Estrades and I practiced."

"There's much more that you need to learn. Her presentation was a minor affair. She is here for one purpose, to be a friend to you as you try to navigate your way through this harsh reality. I say this not to frighten you. I only want to make sure you understand that you will be constantly scrutinized. Remember, the manners of Court are not those of Paris. In fact, the Court establishes its place as distinguished from the rest of France through their ways." He stopped, and snapped his fingers at me. "Don't look overwhelmed, for Versailles is a place of cheerfulness – there is no room for frowns.

And young lady, I can assure you that, come tomorrow evening, you will be most prepared."

He began with a quick review of the nobility and their family connections. This determined how each was addressed, and it was imperative that I make no mistake in my behavior towards them, which would be perceived as a slight. We spoke at length, and he used this time to correct my verbiage, reminding me that the mannerisms and choice of words used at Court are meant to distinguish. Finally, turning to my handmaiden, he explained with precision how to do my hair and makeup, and, nearly imperceptively, placed a few livres in her hand.

"I can assure you that you already have enemies at the Court who would love to embarrass you. It would be far too easy for one of them to convince a servant to play a small trick on you. But soon enough you will know in whom you can trust. Now," he said, turning to the handmaiden, "these are my expectations for Madame de Pompadour on the day of her presentation. If you are wise, you will pay close attention."

Madame d'Estrades waited in my apartment with me while my handmaiden finished. My hair was tightly pulled back and secured, and my face was to be powered white with crimson lips, just as Monsieur de Gontaut instructed. The black gown, the traditional *robe de cour*, was lowered over my head and synched tightly around my back and abdomen, and my finest jewelry was fastened on my neck and wrists.

At exactly ten minutes until 6pm, the Princesse de Conti was announced, and Madame d'Estrades and I stood to follow behind her in a single row, passing through the hallways, and into the salon de l'Oeil de Boeuf. The room was gilded from floor to ceiling in gold with magnificent chandeliers draping from the ceiling. The crowd awaiting us was immense. I abstained from looking around, and instead maintained a smile on my face and focused on taking tiny steps, as Gontaut had instructed, so as to appear as if I were gliding instead of walking. I refused to appear neither overwhelmed nor impressed. It was essential that I looked like I was meant to be here, like I formed part of this world, because soon enough, I would.

We entered the Cabinet du Conseil, where I found the King. I looked into his eyes, and my smile widened. Approaching him, I no longer felt nervous. Dropping my eyes, I bowed deeply to him. But looking up, I could see how uncomfortable he was. He muttered something under his breath that I couldn't understand, and I noticed a slight blush in his cheeks.

But it was alright. I understood him well, and knew that he felt embarrassed. This was not the usual court presentation. His Majesty was presenting his recently ennobled mistress to Court, and everyone recognized me as just that. By choosing me, he had outraged many who didn't appreciate a commoner taking on the position that they felt should be fulfilled by a woman of aristocratic birth. Soon enough, they would come to love me, or at least to endure me, I hoped. Walking backwards, I focused on kicking the train of my gown out of the way and performed three perfectly executed curtsies before exiting his presence.

Walking towards the Queen's rooms, I felt my stomach cramp in knots. After how horribly she had been treated by Madame de Châteauroux, I couldn't imagine what she expected from me, and I feared meeting her.

"Do not expect the Queen to speak more than a few words at your presentation," Madame d'Estrades said. "Remember, you are nothing but a mistress to the King, and the Court looks at you like nothing more than the wife of a *farmer-general*."

Entering her chambers, I bowed as gracefully as I could before her Majesty and ladies-in-waiting. I hoped that, even through this gesture alone, she could sense my deep respect for her.

"I believe you are familiar with Madame de Saissac," she said politely, looking me in the eye. I looked up and stared at her in silent astonishment. She was beginning a conversation with me.

"Yes, your Majesty. I know her from Paris."

"I met her there as well, and found her to be lovely," she went on. Her voice was so gentle, I nearly couldn't make out what she said. But I was overcome with emotion. To everyone's shock, the Queen of France was speaking with me, and at length. Though she was acknowledged as a woman of great dignity, no one expected her to behave with such kindness to me. Overcome with gratitude, I couldn't help but profusely express my deep respect for her, and that I hoped with all of my heart to please her.

The Queen had endured repeated snubs from the King's last favorite, who cruelly didn't care how her behavior alienated the King from his family. I would never be like that woman. Since childhood, the King has been without parents or sibling, and it was because of the Queen that he now had family. I vowed to never be like that woman, his previous lover. Instead, I would do everything in my power to heal the relations with the King and his family that the horrible Madame de Châteauroux had damaged.

CHAPTER XV

It seemed that no sooner had I arrived in Versailles that we set off on *voyage*. The life of the King was one of constant movement. And he was ready to escape the confines of Court. We arrived at one of the King's most beloved residences, the château of Choisy. Escaping the business of Court and the restrictions of its rigidly maintained ceremony, the King was much more at ease here. He encouraged me to invite a few of my friends from Paris, including Charles Pinot Duclos, Voltaire and the abbé Prévost. I was thrilled. Our time at Choisy would be just like my salon in Paris. Here I could mix Parisian intellectuals with aristocracy. It would be a breath of fresh air into the traditional lifestyle of the King's world.

After returning from an afternoon of hunting, I changed out of my hunting outfit, in which I dressed *en amazon,* and joined the King and his comrades for supper. Although the rules were much more lax outside of the palace, my friends were not invited to dine with us. Instead, after supper we joined Voltaire and my friends for cards.

"You won't believe who the Duc de Richelieu brought in tow," whispered Madame d'Estrades.

I looked across the room and saw an average looking woman sitting, just a few years younger than the King, next to Richelieu.

"That," Madame d'Estrades emphasized," is Madame de Châteauroux's sister. Can you believe he had the nerve to bring her here?"

"Hush," I said, showing no reaction. "It's nothing to worry about, let's not feed into the gossip."

Madame d'Estrades raised an eyebrow at my constrained response. She knew very well that this woman's presence would bother me. And of course it did. Why would Richelieu bring her here? It could only be to upset me. He wanted a reaction out of me, a complaint to the King. But I wouldn't give in. The King was in love with me, no other woman would upset me, not now. And I would not trouble him with nagging.

Instead, turning to him, I discussed more pleasant matters.

"Tell me about the château. What makes this your favorite?"

"The grounds," he answered, realistically. "Choisy offers some of the best hunting, and," he went on, smiling, "just down the river is where I met the woman with the most enchanting eyes I've yet to see."

"Is that so," I flirted, "and what makes her eyes so special?"

"Their fire. There's a brilliance to her eyes unlike anything I've ever encountered. And their color, I can't decide if they are blue or green or grey. But it's her eyes that have captured me, and now I can't be without them." I reached under the table and squeezed his hand. "Do you approve of Choisy?"

"I like the grounds," I answered.

"Good. Though," he said, pensively, "I would make some changes to the château."

"Do you feel it's outdated?" I asked, hoping he would agree. "I did have some ideas of how the décor could be modernized." Indeed, I did have a few ideas, though the true purpose of the changes was to erase any memories of the past lovers he has brought here.

"I've seen her work, Sire," said Voltaire, overhearing our conversation. "She has taste fit for a king," he joked.

"She certainly does," the King agreed. "And I believe you do as well. I've read your work. I'm impressed."

Voltaire appreciated the compliment, especially from his Majesty.

"He is the most accomplished writer with the cleverest mind I've met," I said.

"I'd like you to write an opera," announced the King. "I'd like you to portray the battle of Fontenoy."

Voltaire was elated. This opportunity was a great honor for him. Proudly, he bowed his head in appreciation.

One of the King's guests began to discuss plans for the next voyage to Fontainebleau and he turned to answer. But in Voltaire's excitement, he called to the King. Unmoved, the King ignored the interruption, but Voltaire persisted, even tugging on his sleeve! Turning, the King gave him a look as frigid as ice, and Voltaire immediately realized his faux pas. Even worse, the guests noted the faux pas, and began whispering. The King may be kind, but he would never be our equal. I was embarrassed that my friend had treated the King with such familiarity.

I felt so sorry for the awkward moment my dear friend had placed himself in. I knew that proximity to the Crown would launch Voltaire even more. He was an inexhaustible writer, and already received great recognition for his work, but the support of the King would be paramount to his career, and I was determined that the King would promote him into the Academie Française.

That night, lying next to the King, I tried to apologize on behalf of my friend. But as gracious as he was, I knew that it was not wise of me to continue to mix my Parisian friends into his world. I thought I could introduce the freshness of modernity to the tradition of Court, but I was wrong. I couldn't pretend that this was like another salon in Paris. I knew how vulnerable my place in his life was, and the little mistakes of my friends gave his nobles even more reason to mock me and claim that I did not belong in their world. The King loved me, I was certain of it, but our love was so new. I had to win over his inner circle. I had to establish myself in his life. And to truly enter his world, I would have to sacrifice the life I lived before.

Every morning was spent with the King. Undistracted, without pretense, I learned who the man behind the crown was. He loved to hear me tell him stories of my friends in Paris, or silly anecdotes that would make him laugh. He listened as I recited lines from different plays, or sang to him. A courtier wouldn't dream of entertaining him this way, but he loved it, and I was happy to show off my talent. After all, those years learning with Jèliotte and Crébillon needed to be put to use. Here, alone with me, he was happiest and at his ease.

The afternoons, while the King discussed matters of State or hunted, I spent exploring. The grounds of Choisy were vast and the gardens were beautifully maintained and inviting. Wandering towards the river, I looked towards where the King hunted, the Forest of Sénart. It was there that he first took notice of me, and now here I was by his side, and he did not want to be parted from me.

But looking out towards Sénart, I also thought about Etioles and my family there. I missed my mother. I knew she was happy for me, her little *Reinette* now living her destiny and experiencing true love. But now my life was evolving, and I felt the weight of the great chasm that was growing between my family and my life with the King. More than anything, I missed my daughter.

Little Alexandrine was growing. My mother and Monsieur Tournehem wrote letters of her progress, and what a clever little girl she was. But I wasn't there to see her development. Looking back at the château, I felt torn. I wanted to stay here forever, in this perfect paradise, where the King was happy, where we would enjoy the closest thing to a honeymoon we would ever have. And at the same time, I wanted my daughter.

Perhaps, I told myself, I didn't have to choose. If I could establish myself at Court, I could gain the power and influence to afford my daughter a life that one could only dream of. It's decided, I was determined to bring her to Court. The King will love her as I do, and I would raise her to be a great lady, and she would be able to one day marry into nobility. The King, who loved me so dearly, would not make me choose. My Alexandrine, I decided, was even more reason to establish myself at Court.

CHAPTER XVI

After our voyage to Choisy, we stayed at Fontainebleau, but only for a matter of days. Returning to Versailles meant returning to the demands of daily life, a life that I was entirely unaccustomed to.

"Don't leave quite yet," I begged, pulling the King closer to me. "The sun hasn't even risen yet."

Kissing my forehead, he tightened his robe around his waist. "I must. The day begins and my valet will be entering my chamber any moment, and then, the courtiers."

"Then I will rise, too. There's no reason to stay in bed if you are not here with me."

"Today, rest. In two days time, my lovely Marquise, you will join the courtiers in attendance to the Queen. But don't overwhelm yourself. Richelieu mentioned that the schedule, the constant movement, might be too much for you."

I knew Richelieu meant that as an insult. He hoped to make the King doubt that I had the stamina to keep up with the other courtiers. This was yet another way that he tried to make me seem like I didn't belong here. Regardless of how hard I tried to win him over, he was determined to make an enemy out of me.

"How kind of the duke to worry, but I can assure you there is nothing to concern yourself with. I am sure I can keep up."

At Court, every moment of one's existence was predetermined by a constant ritual of daily activities. Such a rigid existence was oppressive for the King, but he refused to undo what his grandfather, Louis XIV, established. The King was a man of tradition, and would honor the customs of his heritage. And so, I too would have to adapt to the exhausting demands of the courtier's schedule.

Just after the sun rose, the King would sneak out of my room and into his own bed before the Valet de Chambre came to wake him. Then, while he washed and shaved, the most revered members of nobility had the honor of attending to him. The ceremony of the *levée*, the King's rising, was terribly important to the courtier. Their rank determined who had the right to hand the King his shirt or his ruffled cuff, for example. The ceremony emphasized their hierarchal position and intimate access to the monarch. It was one of Louis XIV methods of securing the dependence of the courtier on the sovereign.

More courtiers entered to watch him eat breakfast before Mass, although most remained standing while only the high nobility were offered a stool or a seat. In the afternoons, he met with his ministers and dealt with matters of the State. After lunch, he enjoyed a few hours of exercise, usually hunting if weather permitted, before meeting to discuss with his secretary. Finally, the courtiers watched as the King supped with his family, and at nearly midnight, they would attend to the *coucher* ceremony of the King's going to bed.

To me, this custom seemed illogical. Neither the courtiers nor the King could possibly enjoy it. But I was wrong. For the courtiers, these ceremonies allowed them to be near the King, and nearness to the King meant opportunity for advancement and reward. As for the King, he accepted that this was simply a part of his existence. Acknowledging that to be King meant that he had no private life, he often said, "we don't belong to ourselves, but to the public."

Every night, after the official ceremony of the *coucher* was completed, the King joined me in my apartments. Here, with me, he was most content, and that made me feel complete, even valuable. But I didn't want to merely step into the role of a mistress. I wanted to be so much more to him.

"Of course you can," said Madame de Brancas. "There is no need for you to follow in the footsteps of other favorites. You have always been unique."

"But the protocol here, it's unbending. And if I am to be a part of this world, I must abide by its rules."

"I disagree," she teased. "No, you must *know* its rules. But if you are to be irreplaceable, you can't simply step into the role of a courtier. The King loves you, he is at his ease when you are around. Consider his life. He is constantly pulled in different directions, constantly available to the public. His grandfather thrived in this environment, but the King is far more reserved. If it hadn't already become part of tradition, Louis XV would have never instilled such a practice. He is a man that values his privacy, and his few hours of privacy are spent alone with you in your apartments. My advice is this: integrate yourself into his public life."

"I don't see how that is possible."

"Jeanne Antoinette, I have watched you direct salons in Paris and entertain every one of your persnickety guests. Do the same here."

"It's not that simple. This is not Paris. I am barely tolerated here by most."

"It couldn't have been easy to establish your own salon in Paris either," she countered. "But somehow your salon became one of the most sought after by the women of Parisian society."

"Shall I create a salon, then?" I teased.

"That's a brilliant idea. Create a salon, one that revolves entirely around the King."

His days were so demanding, that I knew I had to create an environment where he could find refuge. I took every opportunity to spend time with him, even riding out with him to hunt. The King took pride in having me at his side, his constant companion. Soon, many of his courtiers, especially the younger nobles, came to like me, and I made every effort to win them over. Nevertheless, I still endured the criticism of others.

Madame de Brancas was right, I must recreate a salon. In the *petits cabinets*, I introduced him to the pleasures of the bourgeoisie. The King was most comfortable with small groups of familiar faces, and so I hosted private dinner parties for his closest circle of friends, and with Benoît as my chef, I made sure that every meal was better than the last. Here, in the intimacy of our little club, the King relaxed, and I knew he was growing more dependent on me.

It was only a matter of time before everyone clamored for membership into the little club I had created. Many complained about being excluded, claiming that their position entitled them to enter. But this was an unofficial event, and the rules of hierarchy no longer applied. Instead, the rules were now chosen by me. By limiting access to the King, those that did receive an invitation felt the privilege that I was bestowing on them.

My brother, Abel, frequently joined us. He was my dearest friend, and the King enjoyed his company as well. Richelieu insinuated that the King must be annoyed at my bourgeois family constantly around him, but I learned to pay the duke little mind. The King had, in fact, taken to my brother, and often called him by the nickname I used for him, 'Frèrot' or 'petit frère.'

"When are you going to settle down," I asked Abel one evening after supper. "The King and I have been discussing who would be a good match for you."

"Sister, I am still young. I've no desire to marry yet," Abel said.

Try as I might, I could not persuade Abel to marry, and he couldn't be less interested in benefiting from my position at the King's side. But I was determined to help him. Really, what he was avoiding was becoming a courtier. He loved spending time with us in the *petits cabinets*, but I had to accept that life at Court would stifle him.

Later that evening, when the King and I were alone, I brought up Abel and my concern for his future. "Did you know that Abel is quite talented? Since childhood, we both have had a love of architecture, but Abel far exceeds me in ability." The King was overlooking a few documents that he had brought in to discuss with me. His mind was distracted, but I pursued the matter. "I can scarcely think of a better match for director of *Bâtiments*," I suggested. "After all, the role has been so poorly neglected and could use a fresh perspective."

Still holding his papers in one hand, he looked up at me. The King was disappointed with the minister of finance that had previously fulfilled the role of overseeing the King's Building Works and he had recently been dismissed. The position was available, and Abel would be an excellent choice. The King, I knew, also loved architectural design, and I was sure that this could be another means of entertainment for all of us. With someone as close to me as my own brother in this role, the King and I could be involved in the concept and design of new buildings. Not only would he be more involved in the kind of work that he loved, but we would be working together, as a team.

He hesitated before answering. "He needs experience."

I leaned against him, placing my head on his shoulder and overlooking the documents.

"Perhaps Monsieur Tournehem would be a better fit, at least for the moment. He certainly has enough experience, and he could train Abel," I suggested.

"It would be better if Abel studies in Rome. I will send him there to meet with the ambassador and to gain as much exposure to Italian art and its artists as he can."

The King was right, it would be better if Abel gained his experience abroad. Plus, I hadn't considered the reaction of the nobility, should they discover that my brother, a mere Parisian, had taken the position that they felt should be fulfilled by the aristocracy. Richelieu, in particular, would fuel the flames against me and my family. He disdained us for nothing more than for coming from the bourgeoisie, a class that was progressively gaining power and influence, and this, he saw, was a threat to the aristocracy. In the meantime, the King appointed Monsieur Tournehem for the role, and agreed that when the time came, Abel was to inherit the position.

The King had been very kind to my family, and saw how much I enjoyed their company. I knew it troubled him to not have the same closeness with his own family. His last mistress had done a great deal to strain his relationship with his wife, and this naturally affected his relationship with his children. Of course, the fact that the King had a mistress upset his children, especially his son, the Dauphin, who pouted every time I was in his presence. But there was no other way around it; I was a fixture in his father's life, despite how his son felt about it. The Queen, though perfectly fulfilling her role as monarch and mother, did not fulfill her role as wife. For that reason alone, the King would always have a mistress. But I would not behave like those others and I hoped that they would realize that, if they must accept a mistress, better that it be me than anyone else.

I set about finding ways to repair the relationship between the King and Queen. I recalled the botany lessons my mother gave to me as a child, and worked with the royal gardeners to make arrangements for her Majesty's favorite flowers to be planted. Just as soon as the flowers were in full bloom, they were brought, one dozen after another, to fill her rooms. Overhearing one of her ladies-in-waiting mention that the Queen was greatly concerned about her mounting gambling debts, I eagerly spoke on her behalf to the King. For the first time, he paid her debt. I knew she would see this deed as an olive branch from the King, and that he, too, would feel good at his act of kindness for a woman he had for years been estranged from.

At Fontainebleau, where the rules of etiquette were more relaxed, I took advantage of our time away from Court. Every evening, the King and I joined her to play her favorite game of cards, despite the fact that the game was entirely outdated and no one wanted to play. She was in such good spirits that she spoke and laughed at length with the King and me. I did my best to maintain my composure, to be warm and polite without appearing too familiar. Most importantly, the abyss between them was finally breaking down, and I knew the King was pleased.

The King stepped away to prepare coffee, as he liked to do when he was relaxed. The Duc de Richelieu took notice, as he always did, and came to speak with me.

"It's come to my attention that you have involved yourself in the interior decoration of the Queen's apartments."

He meant this as an accusation. He did not approve of my involvement in royal matters, and did not trust my motives for showing respect to the Queen.

"Nothing of the sort. The Queen has been very kind to me and the King has prepared a surprise for her Majesty," I answered, implying that the King should receive the credit for the act of kindness. "I am sure he would prefer that it remain a surprise."

While at Fontainebleau, I persuaded the King to make arrangements for the Queen's room at Versailles to be re-gilded and a new tapestry with a religious theme to be made for her bed. It was to be set up in her rooms before she returned to the palace. I knew that the Queen would be touched by the gesture. I could never truly be a part of the King's family, but I was sure that if I could help to renew the relationships with his wife and children, he could finally enjoy the family life that he longed for.

"It's a lovely idea, but a rather simple one. She will know it was you, just as she knew that the flowers were sent from you. You really should try to be less obvious. You can't imagine that the Queen of France is pleased to have her husband's mistress, granddaughter of a butcher, begging to gain her favor."

CHAPTER XVII

Fall had come and gone, and the winter was fast approaching. I looked forward to the season with mixed feelings. The snow blanketing the countryside and trees always made Versailles feel romantic, and I loved watching the large, crackling fire with the King. But, without fail, my health suffered during the winter months. The King insisted that I rest and sent his doctors to examine me, but I couldn't just be still and recuperate. It was important to me to attend to my duties to the Queen and pay court to their children.

Every morning the Queen's ladies-in-waiting and I attended Mass. Sitting quietly, I lowered myself to my knees in the Chapel and prayed. Reflecting on my life, on the road I had taken to be here, to be sitting among the nobility with the royal family in the Royal Chapel, firmly established as the favorite of the King, I thought of the many things I had to be grateful for. This moment, I realized, I had achieved what I had longed for during all those years. I had true love, I had the heart of the King.

It was the morning of Christmas Eve, 1745, and I had much to prepare. I had the gifts wrapped and hidden, but I wanted to add a few more decorations before the King visited me this evening. Tomorrow, his time would be spent with his family, so I hoped to make tonight, with no one but us two, our own private Christmas.

"Madame," a soft voice said. I turn to find my handmaiden holding a letter. "It is urgent."

The handwriting belonged to Monsieur Tournehem. Quickly, I open the envelope and read. *Your mother is ill,* it read, *come at once.*

I knew it was grave. My mother would never allow me to leave Court if the matter wasn't serious. Immediately I had my carriage prepared and departed for Paris, where I arrived to find Monsieur Tournehem and my father sitting by her bedside.

"My *Reinette*," she said, a smile warming her ashen face. "I would be cross with Monsieur Tournehem for calling you home, but the doctor says I have very little time left."

Tears filled my eyes, and Tournehem stood up to offer me his seat next to my mother.

"Have they bled you?" I asked.

"Oh yes," she chuckled. "I've been bled and been given all the medicine you could imagine, but it's to no avail. When it's our time, it's our time. And I'd rather enjoy these last few days in peace. Your father and *oncle* Tournehem have waited on me hand and foot. But now," she said, turning to Father, "I'd like a few hours alone with Jeanne Antoinette."

My father kissed her forehead, and the two men shut the door behind them.

"My precious child, my first born, how far you've come," she said, stroking my face with her cool hand. "You have been my greatest pride."

I felt my eyes fill with tears. "Mother, I can't imagine life without you. I feel like I've lost so much time that we could have spent together. This time at Court has taken me from you, and now I can never get that time back."

"Hush, my dear," she said, wiping away my tears and placing her cool hand on my cheek. "We have had more time together than most, and I wouldn't have it any other way. Life's greatest pleasure is to experience lasting love, and that is all I've ever wanted for you."

I felt the cold grip of fear tugging at my heart. I needed my mother. She had always been my strength; I couldn't bear losing her. But she wouldn't let me indulge in my sadness. Instead, she insisted on using this time to council me on my behavior with the King.

I told her of my frustrations with the Duc de Richelieu.

"Ignore that old curmudgeon," she admonished. "You both have a duty to your King, and you have as much purpose in service of the King as the duke. Don't let him ever make you ashamed of where you came from. The bourgeoisie is as much subjects to the King as the aristocracy. Remember, Jeanne Antoinette, always be proud of who you are and where you came from. You are like a breath of fresh air, unlike any other woman the King has met."

I sat awake at my mother's side all night long. Just past midnight, in the early hours of Christmas morning, my mother, my greatest source of wisdom and courage, passed away.

Dawn approached and the carriage slowly made it's way to the palace. A servant gave me his hand to help me down, but I felt so weak that I nearly tumbled to the floor. I felt in a daze, and couldn't remember the journey back to Versailles, or even walking up the stairs to my rooms.

When I entered, I found the King waiting for me. He threw his robe over my shoulders, and wrapped his arms around me. Up until that moment I did everything I could to be strong for my father. I tried to retain my poise in front of the King, but I had no strength left. In the safety of his arms, I cried inconsolably for my mother that I would never see again. My legs gave way, and I nearly collapsed to the floor. Picking me up, he carried me to my bed and held me all night.

The next morning I woke, feeling a ray of sunlight shining through the heavy curtains. My eyes were nearly swollen shut from the tears.

"You must go down for the *levée*," I urged. "Your valet will be in your rooms soon to wake you."

"I will stay here with you today. I don't want to leave your side."

"No, my beloved. You must do your duty, your Court is waiting, and your ministers will need you. Come to me this evening."

The King spent every evening of the next week alone with me. He understood what it meant to loose a loved one, and I was so grateful for his compassion. When he ran out of time to oversee matters with his ministers, he brought the documents upstairs to discuss the matters with me. I became more and more involved in his work, and he trusted my opinion. Unlike others who made suggestions based on personal gain, he knew that my suggestions were based entirely on his best interest.

But I could not allow myself to mourn my mother's passing for long, for it was not permitted in Versailles. Despite the pain of losing my mother, I knew that I must be resilient; the Palace was not a place of compassion, but instead of composure and pleasure. The place of a mistress is always vulnerable, and the courtiers could easily use a moment of weakness to prove that I didn't belong here, or to distract the King with another woman.

Instead I forced myself to refocus my attention on the King and his entertainment. I put my energy into the dinner parties in the *petits cabinets*, where I could enjoy the company of our close friends. Gradually, the sharp pain of the loss of my mother lessened, but when I thought that I would never again see her warm smiling eyes or the comfort of her wisdom, I accepted that the emptiness I now felt would never subside.

Soon enough, there were plenty of distractions to busy my time. The Dauphine was pregnant, and the King was soon to be a grandfather. Although the Dauphin and his wife continued to snub me, their child would be the King's grandchild, and that gave me reason to celebrate. And I had reason to suspect that I may be pregnant too.

"I will be away for a while," the King announced. "But I promise not to be gone long. I want to be here for the birth of my grandson, and return long before you go into confinement," he said, placing his hand on my stomach.

"Must you go?" I begged. "I hate to be parted from you." I wished to come with him, but I understood that, after the Metz affair, he would never allow me to come.

"It's only for a short while. I've made arrangements for you to stay at Choisy for the time being." My pregnancy was barely noticeable, but it was wise to avoid the attention and Court gossip, especially without the King. "But I will be back before the end of the Spring. I have something that needs your attention," he said coyly, handing me a large scroll of paper.

"What's this?" I asked, stretching out the stroll to find architectural plans.

"This is Crécy, my gift for you," he smiled, and took the plans from me to lie on the desk before us. "Pâris Montmartel was a great help to me in acquiring the property, and wisely bought it under your name. There's no need to upset the ministers or provoke them into thinking that I am spending frivolously. But this is my gift to you. You'll see that there's much work that needs to go into it. For that reason alone, I knew you would love it. It will be your project."

I held his face in my hands and kissed him. "You know me so well. Thank you, my love."

The next few weeks I spent at Crécy with Monsieur Tournehem. Tournehem was connected with France's finest architect and designers, and together he and I worked hand in hand with them. All of the other royal lodgings had been marred by memories of the King's past favorites. Many were outdated and in need of renovation. Crécy would be entirely distinct. Crécy would be our own, and I had a vision of what I wanted the château to be. Here, I would create an estate, a private refuge that served the sole purpose of entertaining the King in a way that only I could.

Six weeks later, I received a letter from the King. He was to return to Versailles. I arranged for my things to be prepared at once so that I could be back at the palace before he arrived to welcome him.

Impatiently I waited in my rooms at Versailles until finally I could hear the horses approach. Looking out my window I found the servants forming a perfect line, dressed in their fine livery, and his ministers and the royal family gathered to welcome him home. But I didn't go down. Instead I sat there, fidgeting with the hem of my gown, anxiously awaiting for him to enter my rooms. I needed to speak with the King alone.

"I'm sorry I didn't tell you this sooner," I said, looking away from him. "But I thought it best to tell you in person. I've lost the child."

He took both of my hands into his own. "Don't cry," he said, tenderly wiping away the tears on my cheek. "We can soon try for another."

"I am afraid...I don't think I can carry any more children." Admitting this made me feel as if a part of me died. I placed my hands on my womb, my now empty womb where, only a week ago I felt the little fluttering of our child moving. "All I've ever wanted was to be near you, to share a life together. And to have a child with you, it would mean that we've created a family together. I wanted to give that to you."

I rested my head on his shoulder, and he placed his hand under my chin. "Look at me," he said, his breath warm against my hair.

I shook my head. "My face is red and blotchy, I don't want you to see me like this."

"You are beautiful, let me look at you. My darling, you must remember, you and I *are* a family. And we share a life together. Jeanne Antoinette, every evening after retiring from work, and every morning when I open my eyes, it is you that I seek. You understand me, and accept me for the man that I am. No one I've ever had in my life has meant to me what you have. I've never been loved the way you love me. Having a child would not change what you mean to me."

CHAPTER XVIII

In the middle of the July heat of 1746, the Dauphine went into labor. The King's ministers and the Princes of the Blood reclined in the satin chairs, watching the Dauphin nervously pace back and forth, his hands clasped behind his back. The King stood by the window. He wished he could comfort his son, but knew there was little he could do to calm his anxiety. Finally, a lady-in-waiting entered.

"The Dauphine has given birth," she announced. "A girl." The kingdom, of course, hoped for a son, another heir, but the Dauphin couldn't have been happier. He was a man in love, and he had a family. A son could come next year, today he would celebrate his wife and child.

His joy was not to last.

"I'm sure you've heard," said the King, entering my rooms that evening. "Our Dauphine has passed."

"Yes, Sire. I am so very sorry." My handmaiden informed me that morning that the Dauphine's health, which seemed strong after giving birth, was quickly failing. There was nothing the doctors could do to prevent it.

"My son," he said, shaking his head. "He is inconsolable. And I feel helpless to comfort him. I've never seen him like this. He was clutching at her corpse," he said, horrified at what he witnessed. "I had to drag him away from her."

"You are a good father, my darling," I reassured him. "There was nothing more you could have done."

"I understood him in that moment more than ever before. He had a love that was priceless, he had something that was irreplaceable, and now he has lost her forever."

After the mourning ceremonies and the midnight procession to the royal burial at the mausoleum of St. Denis, the Dauphine was laid to rest. It seemed as if all of Versailles, from the courtiers to the curtains, was covered in black. The atmosphere was morose, and the King's mood turned morose with it. Once again, the time came to travel to the royal chateaus, and we left for Choisy.

I thought the voyage away from Court would be a welcome change, a way to distract the King from the melancholy of the death of his daughter-in-law. But even here we couldn't find peace of mind. There was hardly any room for the great party that accompanied us, and even away from Court, the silly disputes from nobles back at Versailles over hierarchal rights were a constant annoyance. I could see the King was growing more and more frustrated. I needed to find a way to distract him.

Leaning against his chair, his chin resting on his hand, the King sat reading the letter from the Maréchal de Saxe, the great general of Fontenoy and friend of the Pâris brothers.

"Any news?" I asked. The King had been talking about joining the Maréchal and going back to the army, and I wanted to find a way to prevent another separation from him.

He sighed deeply. "He says that all is well. There's no need of me there." It appeared that de Saxe had indeed received my note, requesting that he not encourage the King's departure.

I exhaled, relieved at the news.

"In that case, why don't you join me at Crécy? My brother has sent me several sketches from Italy for the estate that must be reviewed, and Tournehem has written me. He is still there, working very closely with our architect. I'm very lucky to have the expertise of Monsieur Lassurance. He has been so kind as to oversee the architectural restructuring in its entirety, which I assure you is no small feat. But the plans need to be approved, and I'd love for you to help me with them."

I organized for Madame d'Estrades and several other women in our party to leave the next morning for Crécy, and the men would join us later. There was much to do to prepare. I had never had the King as a guest in my estate before, but I was sure he would enjoy himself. After all, every aspect of the architecture and design of the grounds was meant to entertain him. And there was no better timing to distract him from his troubles than now.

The château had been under heavy construction for months, and had been visited by no one but our architect Lassurance, Tournehem, and dozens of laborers. Despite my distance from the estate, I had been involved in every aspect of its renovation. Tournehem and Lassurance reviewed the sketches Abel sent me from Rome that I wished to be included in the design. I adored the Italian rococo style, and implored my brother to constantly study the classical architecture and décor. France had some of the best craftsmen in the world, and rococo was a style I was sure would be a success. Despite some hesitation at first, Lassurance confirmed that it could be included in his plans.

By the time the King and his small entourage of men arrived, the house was made perfectly comfortable. Still, I made sure that there were many different projects focused on the design of the house for the King to involve himself with. Upon arrival, I gave him a tour of all the work that had been completed.

"Look there," I said, pointing to the two new wings of the château. "They've nearly finished with the construction on both sides! And there, overlooking the river, look what they've done there," I said, pointing to the amphitheatre. "That was at your suggestion."

I could sense that his mood was beginning to lighten. Finally, he had found something new to interest him. My chef Benoît prepared lunch for us, and the King spent the meal discussing his ideas with Tournehem and Lassarance. While the King was concerning himself with the stables, the view from the terrace overlooking the river and the village below, and the uniforms to be worn by all male guests, I was focused on the artwork. During my childhood, the Pâris Brothers had constantly reminded me of the value of art, and the importance of supporting French artists. This home would be an excellent means of supporting the work of the Frenchman. The King, of course, also took interest in the cultural aspects of his country, but those matters usually received less attention than his primary distractions of politics and hunting.

Our time together at Crécy made me realize that the King had been so absorbed in matters of the State that his main outlet of escape from the mundane monotony and demand of duty was hunting. But here, away from Court and it's routine, it was obvious that he had discovered another form of enjoyment, one in which we could explore together. I had work from some of Paris' finest artists brought in and displayed in different rooms, and he made suggestions of what decorations would be most suitable. He even drew up plans for a roof garden, and had rare plants brought in.

We returned to Versailles shortly thereafter. Here, during our evenings together, he worked on new designs, reviewed the most recent illustrations Abel sent from Italy, and discussed other properties he thought of acquiring and renovating. Of course, he also brought up documents that his ministers had given him for review. Now, he nearly always discussed the matters of policy with me, and often left the documents on my desk for me to review in the morning.

The King was typically a shy, rather reserved man, especially around unfamiliar faces. But when we were alone, he smiled and laughed. I always searched for fun little means of entertaining him. He loved to hear jokes and gossip, and was especially amused when I would read reports from Paris to him. Recalling my lessons from Jèloitte, I recited bits of plays, or sang for him. I soon realized that, through entertainment, I remained the center of comfort in his increasingly demanding world.

"In you I've found everything a man could dream of," he would often say. With me, he had a friend and partner that could ride alongside him during the hunt, someone to make him laugh, who he could discuss the complexities of politics with, a woman he could sit by the fire and relax with after a long day. But there was one thing I knew I was failing at.

"You can't be serious," Madame de Brancas scolded, looking at my plate of celery and truffles. "This is what Benoît has prepared for today?"

"It's meant to be good for my health," I said, defensively.

"Exactly," Madame d'Estrades agreed, "they say it's a wonderful aphrodisiac."

"I doubt this is what Dr. Quesnay prescribed for you," lectured Madame de Brancas, and ordered Madame du Hausset, my new *femme de chamber,* to have a proper lunch prepared for me.

I didn't like that Madame de Brancas treated me like a child. I needed help. I needed something to make me desire intimacy.

"I'm going to lose him," I cried. "It's only natural for a king to want to be intimate, but he wants more than I am able to give. I can't keep up any longer. This constant movement, it is exhausting, and now it's taking its toll on my health. Every morning we wake by 8am, then off to Mass, then I pay court to the Queen and her children. Most evenings I host private supper parties, and the King and I don't fall asleep until 3am. I have a constant stream of visitors who require I speak on their behalf to the King, correspondences to respond to, or a voyage we are preparing to leave for." The pace was more than I could endure, but I had no choice. This was the life I had chosen.

"None of the elixirs worked?" asked Madame d'Estrades.

I sighed deeply. "Nothing. Dr. Quesnay visits me a few times a week, and he has found no remedy. It's hopeless."

"Some women are just naturally colder," she replied, shrugging her shoulders. It was true, I was just a naturally cold woman. I had the love of a king, and I was going to lose him.

"That's absolutely ridiculous," Madame de Brancas said flatly, making a stern face at Madame d'Estrades. "Don't put such ideas into her head. Remember how well you felt that summer you spent in Etioles? Your diet was full of food in its most natural form. That's the best thing for you."

"It won't work. Even when my health is at it's strongest, I lack desire. I'm going to lose him."

"Listen to me," she said. "The King needs you in his life. You have become a great source of strength for him, and he depends on you."

"He will replace me. There are too many young women that are poised at taking my place, and too many courtiers that would love to watch my fall." Madame d'Estrades' eyes widened. I knew she loved her position at Court, and enjoyed her growing prominence. Recently I had found her a position as a lady-in-waiting to one of the King's daughters, a role that delivered both esteem and great profit to her. If another were to take my place, she knew just as well as I did that she would lose her position as well.

"He could never, never replace you. There is no other woman in all his life that fulfills him the way you do. You are indispensable to him."

"She's right, though," warned Madame d'Estrades to Madame de Brancas. "He could very well take another lover." Turning to me, she said, "Forgive me, but I say this to you only to prepare you."

"He may," countered Madame de Brancas, always in control. "But another lover does not mean another favorite, it doesn't mean that you've lost your place in his heart. My suggestion," she said, softening her voice, "is this. Simply continue to do what you do best. Love him unconditionally. Let him feel accepted just as he is, without guilt or disappointment. Madame, I can guarantee that he has never met a woman that is as charming as you, or one that makes him as happy and content as you do. You, above all his courtiers, know how to please him."

I was determined that this lacking in my nature would not take the King from me. Instead I doubled my efforts to be the partner that he needed.

CHAPTER XIX

Pleasure was at the heart of Versailles. Boredom was intolerable. But the weather that winter of 1747 had quickly turned, making it impossible for the King to find distraction in hunting. With no outlet to distract him, his mood, as I feared, grew more and more impatient. Even the various forms of entertainment that had been overseen by the Duc de Richelieu became repetitive, uneventful.

"It's time for a fresh form of amusement, don't you think," I said lightheartedly to him one morning. "I've been working on a surprise for you, something I know you will love."

"Whatever you like, *ma cherie*," he said absentmindedly, standing to wrap the robe around himself and making his way to the staircase for the *levée*. "Whatever makes you happy."

I was bothered that he hadn't stayed to talk with me. This new project was exciting, and I wanted to discuss with him more. I feared he was growing distant, that something was distracting him from me.

"Sometimes, my friend," said Madame de Brancas, "you astound me. I still can't imagine how you managed to pull this together." The courtiers were reading over their scripts that Madame du Hausset, my new *femme de chambre*, had delivered to them in envelopes labeled "confidential," and now, the small cast of us were all gathered at Choisy to rehearse in private.

"I just hope the King doesn't find out what we are up to. It's impossible to keep anything a secret in Versailles, and this *must* be a surprise." I looked across the room at the seamstresses who worked under the great designer Perronet, while they took the measurements of the Marquis de Gontaut. Perronet brought boxes of sample fabrics, lace, and ribbons with him, and I still needed to approve his designs for the costumes before the end of the day. There never seemed to be enough time, but at the same time, I loved the excitement.

"I'm sure his Majesty will have no idea what you're up to," she promised reassuringly. "When do the members of the *Comédie Française* arrive?"

"Shortly, I hope. I've made sure that every one of the actors from our cast has had experience acting or singing, but most haven't had nearly as much experience as you or I."

"Of course not. Certainly they frequent the theatre, but it is only in Paris or in their countryside estates that they would have a private theatre to perform at. It will be good to have the expertise of professional actors."

"I'm certainly indebted to the *Comédie Française*," I said, and thought back on my singing lessons as a little girl with Jéliotte, one of the most famous performers of the *Comédie Française*. "They are even sending over members from their orchestra to work with the Duc de Chaulnes and Monsieur de Sourches and their servants. I must think of a gift to thank them."

"I'm sure they were more than happy to oblige," she said, laughing lightheartedly. "Performing a favor for the King's favorite, the most powerful woman in France, ensures that you will return them in kind. They couldn't possibly refuse such a request. And you, Madame, have exceeded yourself at yet another novel means of pleasing the King."

I hoped she was right. My theatre at Etioles had always been a success, and I hoped the King would enjoy my performance as much as I enjoyed performing. I was an accomplished amateur actress, and I wanted him to finally see all the effort I had put into preparing to be worthy of a king since my earliest years. I wanted so badly to again be the center of his attention, the source of his enjoyment. But I also feared that he would find my theatre to be bourgeois and unworthy of his courtiers that now served as actors.

"Madame de Pompadour," came the concerned voice of Duc de la Vallière, "I doubt there is enough space here to perform."

"Of course, monsieur, I was thinking the same thing. No, we could not possibly hope to perform here. This is merely a location away from Court for us to rehearse. The King has allowed me to decorate the gallery near the Cabinets des Médailles, though he has no idea what I'll be using the space for. Boucher and Pérot are there now painting and embellishing."

Vallière nodded his head in approval. To have such distinguished artists as Boucher and Pérot decorating the stage signified that the performance was no small matter, and to be among the few chosen to perform before the King represented that the courtiers acting in the play were an acknowledged and privileged elite.

"How long will you be sending the astronomers to Peru and Mexico?" I asked the King.

"Pardon?"

"The astronomers, how long will they need to be abroad to make observations of the heavens? It was a brilliant idea of you to send them. You know, I was very pleased to hear the Doctor express his great respect for what you are doing for this age through your support of the progress of science." I said, but the King didn't respond. "Darling, is everything alright? All through dinner you seemed like your mind was entirely elsewhere."

"Yes, it's nothing. I don't want you concerned with it," he answered, but his voice sounded strained, worried. I could tell that whatever the matter was, he was greatly upset by it.

"Please tell me what it is. It troubles me more to know that there is something that worries you that you feel your can't share with me, and it gives me such comfort when you express your concerns with me," I promised, hoping to reassure him.

"It's a matter that merely needs to be handled, and I would rather it remain private."

This was entirely unlike him. The King had complete confidence in me, with both personal and political matters. And now he was pulling away. Whatever was plaguing him, I was determined to find out what it was.

"My beloved, I can see that you are trying to protect me from something. But I can assure you, you do me more harm be censoring me from it than from relieving yourself of this burden and letting me help you."

He stood and walked to the window, sighing deeply before admitting what was on his mind. "There's a young woman, a girl really," he began, avoiding looking me in the eyes. "She is pregnant."

I understood immediately. My health had recently made it impossible for me to have the sexual stamina needed to please the King, and so he had satisfied his pleasures elsewhere.

Leaning forward, I picked up a crystal water glass and drank. I needed a moment to regain my composure before reacting. I would not let him see how deeply his infidelity tore at my heart, and I refused to punish him for my inability to meet his needs. I understood what he needed at this moment was not a mistress, but a counselor that could think rationally and without emotion, and unlike the other courtiers, I was the only one that wouldn't use this as an opportunity to gain leverage with the King.

"Does the young lady know who the father is?" I asked, hoping I seemed unaffected.

"To her knowledge, the father is a wealthy nobleman from Poland, of some relation to the Queen."

I walked over to him and rubbed his back. "That was very clever, it's better that she doesn't know your identity." Already, he was relieved, and I was glad to be kept in his confidences. Once the King could see that he could share all the details with me without being made to feel remorse or shame, he told me everything.

"Madame de Hausset," I called, and she entered immediately. "My dear, I have a great favor that I must ask of you."

"Of course, Madame."

"There is a house on the Avenue de St. Cloud. There, you will find a young woman who is with child. You must take charge of the house, oversee the birth, and name the parents at the baptism. She believes the father to be a Polish nobleman. Don't let her think otherwise. It is imperative that we avoid attracting attention, or that this is in any way linked to his Majesty." I walked to my cabinet, and opened a small, finely carved wooden box that contained a small but fine diamond. "Take this, a gift for the mother," I instructed. "It must not be too large, or else it would attract attention." I said, and the King nodded in approval. "Above all, be sure that this remains secret, as the King wishes."

Once alone, the King turned towards me, and I could see the remorse in his beautiful brown eyes.

"You are my dearest friend, and I want you to always come to me without fear, and share with me what troubles you. Nothing will make me feel more invaluable to you," I assured him.

"I am so sorry, I would never want you to know about this."

His eyes filled with tears, as did mine, and I placed my hand on his heart. "It is but your heart that I want."

The King was having romantic trysts. I had more sources inform me of them than I wanted to hear. He had been regularly frequenting the young mistresses who were all accommodated in a large house, known as the Parc aux Cerfs, on the outskirts of Versailles, and there was nothing I could do to prevent it. The fear of losing him tore at me, and my anxiety resulted in another miscarriage.

Gossip of the establishment swarmed through the palace, and courtiers snickered that, at the Parc aux Cerfs, or "park of the stag," the King hunted more than in the forest. The Marquis d'Argenson, in particular, made vulgar insinuations that the mansion was the King's harem of prostitutes, and claimed I was its ringleader. He crudely wanted to paint me as the depraved favorite that sought wanton decadence as new means of pleasuring the King. Nothing could be further from the truth.

Even Doctor Quesnay expressed his concern for how often the King made visits to the young women. But as much as I tried to satisfy the King, my health wouldn't permit it. If I wanted to share my life with him, I would have to accept that I lacked the ability to gratify his appetite for intimacy. It was a reality I had done everything to avoid.

I had failed him. The King's infidelities made me feel powerless, incapable of realizing my role as the partner in his life that I tried so hard to be. I was unable to fulfill him. But if I were to keep him, I would have to turn a blind eye, hold my tongue from rebuking him, and accept him as he was. My role in his life, if I were going to keep my place as his favorite, must evolve.

Instead of dwelling on the vulnerability that I felt as a *maîtresse* that couldn't please her lover, I refocused my efforts on the qualities that bound him to me, and threw myself into perfecting my performance in the play.

Within weeks our cast was prepared, and we set the date of the first performance, that of Molière's *Tartuffe*, for the 17th of January. Only fourteen were invited to attend our performance, and I made sure that each member of the audience, as well as the actors, was of the King's close friends, in whose company he was most at ease.

As much as I tried to keep our performance a secret, many courtiers discovered our plan soon enough. Never wanting to lose an opportunity of the close contact with the King that a private event promised, courtiers clamored for an invitation. Even Madame du Hausset requested a part in the play for a courtier. The young man for whom she spoke on behalf of promised to give her close relative a position of command in exchange for a minor role in the play. It was a small request, and I could refuse my loyal *femme de chambre* nothing. But other than that, I made no exceptions.

Madame du Hausset hurried to my side. "The King has already arrived," she said. "And most of the audience has entered with him."

"He must have left his hunt early," I thought aloud. "That's unusual for him, he never leaves a day of hunting early."

"But he would for you, Jeanne Antoinette. He knows how important this is to you, and you are important to him," said Madame de Brancas. She was the only one I dared to share the incident of the young pregnant girl with, and she knew how deeply insecure I felt.

"The two actresses that arrived late are nearly ready," said Madame du Hausset.

"In future, I will have to establish a set of rules for our theatre. I don't like that the King is expected to wait because of their tardiness."

The King's manservant approached, and I worried that the King was growing impatient.

"Please tell his Majesty that we are nearly ready," I began.

He handed me a note, gave a slight bow, and returned to his chair.

I eagerly await to behold you with my eyes, and later in my arms, it read.

Our entire cast poured themselves into their characters, delivering each line with profound emotion and wit, bringing the audience to genuine laughter. By the end of the performance, the King stood and with a hearty applause, he shouted, "You are the most delicious woman in all of France."

Madame de Brancas put her arm lovingly around my waist. "You see, he's never been more in love."

"The Duc de Richelieu is furious," announced Madame d'Estrades. "It has been his privilege to arrange *Les Menus'* entertainments for the King. Why didn't you consult with him before you began the plays?"

"Yes," I said, unfazed at her alarm. "The King mentioned the duke's complaints. He is outraged that a mistress of the middle class has dared to take his place."

"Perhaps it would be wise to retire from the theatre so that the duke can resume his role as director."

I looked up from my letters, surprised at her defense of Richelieu. There was a change that had taken place in Madame d'Estrades, but I couldn't place my finger on what it was.

"If the King had been entertained by the Duc de Richelieu's monotonous schedule of the *Comédie Italienne,* then the *Comédie Française* every week without variation, there would be no need for my efforts. But Richelieu has grown lax in his responsibilities to amuse the King, thus he prefers that I manage his entertainment. I don't see why Richelieu feels entitled to protest."

"I imagine you feel susceptible – if Son Excellence is bored, he will find his pleasure elsewhere. But don't you think it is a great risk to make an enemy out of the Richelieu?"

"The Duc de Richelieu," interrupted Madame de Brancas, "has found reason to complain of Jeanne Antoinette since he first met her. Let's not forget that he enjoyed a great deal of control over Madame de Châteauroux, and must now be frustrated at having no favor with the Marquise. Perhaps he should be less concerned about the pleasure the King clearly enjoys from Madame's theatre, and more concerned with making an enemy out of the one whom the King trusts most."

Madame de Brancas never cared for my cousin, Madame d'Estrades, and often warned me that she was jealous of my social elevation into the nobility, when, prior to becoming the *maîtresse en titre* to the King, she was of a superior social class to me.

"Thank you for your warning, dear friend. I know you have my very best interest at heart," I said to Madame d'Estrades, hoping to smooth the mounting tension between the two women. "But the King finds great enjoyment in the performances. And should he feel any inclination to have Richelieu resume the responsibilities of *Les Menus*, he would find me more than willing to oblige and obey."

It was only a matter of time until Richelieu, in his insecurities of losing his position as director of royal entertainer to a bourgeois, took matters into his own hands. Without permission from the King, he declared that neither the musicians nor the workmen were permitted to work for me. The entire cast, who was apprised of this while on their way to rehearsal, was furious. I addressed Richelieu's defiance directly to the King.

That evening, sitting with the courtiers in the *petits cabinets*, I had to suffer the duke's laughter and tails about his campaign, and both the King and I behaved as if nothing was the matter. That night Richelieu, who was First Gentleman of the Bedchamber, prepared the King for bed.

"How many times have you been to the Bastille," asked the King, referring to the numerous occasions that the duke had been imprisoned.

"Three, your Majesty."

The King, who often times, was a man of few words, need say no more. Richelieu understood that a threat to the King's favorite was far more dangerous than he thought. Richelieu now realized, as would the other courtiers soon enough, I was not to be underestimated.

CHAPTER XX

"Parliament is insistent that the Dauphin marry again, and soon," the King said, handing me my playing cards.

"Do you feel the timing is right?" I asked, looking at the hand he dealt me.

"I admit, I have to agree with them. He needs to produce an heir. Time is precious and we've no time to lose. It's his responsibility as the future King of France, and as my only son, his responsibility holds even greater weight. But he still mourns the loss of his wife, and I would rather not put more pressure on him at this time."

"The Dauphin could have no better papa," I said, smiling. "Have you spoken to him about the matter?"

"Briefly. He has an inclination towards the Infanta Antonia of Spain. But that's an impossible match, she is his wife's sister."

"I'm sure such a fondness for the Infanta is only because she reminds him of her sister. The Dauphin was devastated by her death," I said, knowing full well that a marriage to the sister of the first Dauphine would never be accepted in Paris. It would seem too similar to incest. "What are his other options?"

He handed me a list of young royals that would be prospective brides for his son.

"It's a rather short list," I noted.

The King sighed. "There are very few possibilities for him," he admitted with disappointed. "I don't want to force him to marry when there are so few to choose from."

"Sire," I said gently, placing my hand on top of his. "Remember, you were in a similar circumstance when you married the Queen, and she has secured your legacy and blessed France with many children."

I scanned through the short list of princesses and the many details supporting or opposing their candidacy. I knew that the King was frustrated with listening to the arguments of his ministers for one princess or another, and truly there were very few women to choose from.

"Marie-Josèphe," I announced, recognizing the name.

"Yes, I noticed her as well. She is the niece of the Maréchal de Saxe." The maréchal was a friend, one whom both the King and I had the highest regard for. As soon as I realized his niece could be the future Dauphine, I knew that was the candidate I wanted to support. "She crossed my mind, as well. It would please me to honor the Maréchal de Saxe through this marriage. Few have served France with such loyalty and ardor as he," he said, referring to the great victory against the British that the maréchal had won at the battle of Raucoux. "But she would not be a good choice." The King stood to pour a glass of wine. "Or rather, I should say she would be a controversial choice."

"Of course," I realized immediately what he was referring to. She was the daughter of Augustus III, the man who dethroned the Queen's father from his rule over Poland. But I couldn't abandon this opportunity quite so easily. The maréchal was a man I wanted to see elevated, particularly since he had had to endure conducting war alongside the insufferably prideful Prince de Conti, cousin of the King. Regardless of my efforts to befriend him, Conti was endlessly rude to me. And since he had been promoted to supreme general, it seemed only fair that we reward Saxe, as well. "I would hate to upset her Majesty, I assure you. But when we consider how few options there are, and that the Princess of Saxony is but fifteen-years-old and comes from a family with many children, it seems that she is the most promising option we have. With her, there is the highest likelihood of a fruitful marriage and many babies."

"Only you can present an argument that I cannot refuse," he said, smiling. "Do you remember the Dauphin's first wedding?"

"How could I forget? I dressed as your favorite goddess that evening, the goddess of the hunt. And you, dressed identically with all your men, as tall green yew trees. But I knew exactly which one you were," I said, stroking his face with my hand.

"Impossible," he laughed.

"Not so," I countered playfully, sitting up straight and looking him in the eyes. "I knew who you were by the way you looked at me.

No one makes me feel the way you do just by looking at me." He took my hand in his and turned it to kiss the inside of my palm.

"I will make the arrangements, and send Richelieu to escort the Saxon princess to Court. As for the Dauphin's wedding, Richelieu won't be handing that this time. Instead, I am counting on you to oversee the details, particularly the list of invitations."

More and more, the King trusted me to undertake key responsibilities and decisions. He spent every evening with me, and in the privacy of my rooms, we discussed everything together. Both courtiers and dignitaries visited me nearly every day to beg that I speak on their behalf or present the King with their concern. Rarely was a promotion or favor granted without my action as an intermediary; rarely was a minister dismissed or replaced without my suggestion of the replacement. The King, having a million responsibilities already, took great comfort in knowing that I could fulfill this role for him, and felt confident that, unlike his other advisors, I was without ambition and entirely devoted to his best interest.

I was, now, indispensable to the King. There was not one who understood him the way that I did, that innately knew what he needed, that could smooth over the awkward moments he found himself in due to his shyness, or entertain him and make him laugh the way that I did. I knew all his preferences and habits. The courtiers no longer dared to treat me as their social inferior. Instead, they found that I was a source of influence they would be wise to attach themselves to. And though I could not assuage the disapproval my enemies felt for me as a bourgeoisie that had gained power in the world of the aristocracy, they now realized that I was to be treated with deference.

As my role as *maîtresse en titre* grew more and more demanding, it was inevitable that my health suffered. After completing five years of Théâtre des Petits Cabinets, Doctor Quesnay ordered that I discontinue such wearisome forms of entertainment. Still, my headaches worsened and I frequently found myself incapacitated by a fever or a cold. The King and I continued to try to have children, but every time I became pregnant, within weeks I lost the child. I convinced the Doctor to move to Versailles, where he could treat me nearly every day to check my health. Finally, it was determined that I could no longer sleep with the King.

For so long I'd feared the day that I could no longer be intimate with the one man I had dedicated my life to. Despite the fact that the King continued to spend every evening with me, I knew that it was out of the comfort of my company, and our relationship had developed into a friendship. I could no longer fulfill my place as the sole companion in his life. And I knew, just as well as everyone else at Court that he continued to visit his "little birds" at the Parc aux Cerfs.

There was one woman in particular that had caught his eye, and I knew she had become his lover. But what right did I have to punish him? He was not only a king, but a Bourbon. Although he wasn't as licentious as his grandfather, Louis XIV, who would sleep with the *femme de chamber* if his mistress took too long to undress, Louis XV was an incredibly virile gentleman. He, just like his forefathers, required intimacy – an intimacy that I could no longer provide for him. But I knew in my heart that he would not abandon me, not for one of those young, uneducated beauties. Instead, I accepted the situation just as it was, and enjoyed him despite the hurt that the infidelity caused me.

Anyway, it was my fault that he had even noticed her. Before gaining the King's attention, she was nothing more than a young Irish beauty who my most favored artist, François Boucher had taken an interest in, and she soon after became his muse. The young lady was blessed with an angelic face that Boucher captured so well. So as a gift to the Queen, I commissioned Boucher to use her as a model and to paint the Holy Family. Now, not only did the painting draw in the attention of the King, but the Queen had to look on at the face of her husband's new lover. Proud to flaunt her new status as the King's lover, *La Morphil*, as she was nicknamed, was not one to hide behind closed doors. Instead, she was often seen on Sunday attending church or walking in the park. Within a matter of time she became pregnant. Still, I refused to allow myself to worry.

And then, one day in mid June, my entire world stopped. I received a letter from the convent where my daughter, my precious Alexandrine, was being educated. She had been arrested by convulsions, there was nothing that could be done. My daughter, at just ten years old, had died.

I can't express the pain of a mother losing their only child. The world, after that moment, never seemed as bright; I knew it would never bear the brilliance that it once held.

I ordered Madame du Hausset to close the curtains. For days I remained in darkness, and saw no one but the King. But there was no comfort he could bring me. Nothing would bring my daughter back. My father, who loved that child so very dearly, died of heartbreak just four days later. I was now an orphan. The King, and my brother Abel, were all I had left.

The King refused to leave my side, weeping with me and holding me as we mourned together for my little "Fan-Fan." He felt the loss of Alexandrine nearly as much as I did. It was because of him that she was able to enroll in the prestigious *convent des Dames de l'Assomption*, located relatively close to home in Paris. Here, growing alongside the little girls and young ladies of the highest echelons of nobility, she received the finest education – an upbringing that was meant to prepare her for a noble marriage, which I had arranged for her to the son of the Duc de Picquingy. I was so looking forward to her marriage, and to sharing her life at Court with me. Little Fan-Fan visited Versailles often, and the King, who had many daughters of his own, took great delight in my little girl. We watched her grow from a child to a young woman. Now she was gone, and her future, which I had done so much to secure, died with her.

My tears dried. I had not more tears to cry. Instead I sat stoic, lifeless, staring out the window. And by my side he stayed, refusing to allow me to endure my heartbreak alone. Finally, I begged him to take a few hours each day and return to his duties. France could not afford for him to neglect his responsibilities, I reminded him.

Soon after I heard that Louise O'Murphy had been married off to an officer. Madame du Hausset, who, like most servants, was always well-informed of Court gossip, apprised me of the sudden break. During one of the King's visits, she had asked him about our relationship, referring to me as his "vieille coquette," the old flirt. It was the last time she would see him.

I may no longer be the King's lover, but he would never let another, whether trusted courtier or lover, degrade the woman that had relentlessly stood by his side. The King and I had already been through so much together, we were a part of each other's lives. I had grown into the very fabric that made him who he was. We had truly become a family. Despite what the courtiers who hated me, and the mistresses who hoped to unseat me assumed, I would not be replaced. But I did accept that my role in the King's life had forever changed. I accepted that no longer was I his lover - but his friend, his confidant, his most trusted advisor – that I would be.

And with this new position in his life, I decided it was time to change apartments. I took those that previously belonged to Madame de Montespan, the lover of Louis XIV. The rooms were old, and were in great need of updating. This, as well as the private staircase that connected the King's rooms to my own, was the primary reason for moving to these new apartments. Here, he could have private access to me, and came up at all hours to be alone with me. *Oncle* Tournehem took charge of overseeing the reconstruction of the rooms, and though he was incredibly diligent, the project seemed to take much longer than necessary. Finally, just after Christmas, I was able to move in. And yet, despite how deep our bond of friendship grew, every night I lay in bed, fearing the day another would take my place.

CHAPTER XXI

Madame d'Estrades joined me for a walk through the exquisite gardens of Versailles. The sun was bright, and a servant walked behind us with a large umbrella, high above our heads. The gardens were magnificent, and Louis XIV had done well in ensuring that their splendor was unrivaled by any other palace. I smiled to myself to think that, at only twenty-seven years old, the King's grandfather decided to develop a swampy, mosquito infested land where his father's hunting lodge was located, into what is now the palace of Versailles. With this building, Louis XIV created a legacy, and now, I wanted to ensure that the King, too, created for himself a legacy just as grand.

"It seemed that the King was very amused at the wedding you hosted at Crécy," Madame d'Estrades said. "It is exceedingly kind of you to organize such an extravagant wedding for simple country girls."

"I rather enjoy it, actually, and it didn't seem to be too extravagant."

She laughed, placing her hand on my arm. "You finished the evening with fireworks, and each girl was gifted with a more than generous dowry."

"A wedding should be the best night of a woman's life, and it pleases the King and me to make the occasion special. After all, these young ladies live on my estates, it's only natural that I feel responsible to host their wedding. And the King really does enjoy weddings. I am sure he is looking forward to the wedding of your niece."

"She is greatly indebted to you, Madame. I cannot thank you enough for using your influence to arrange the wedding between my Charlotte-Rosalie, and the Comte de Choiseul-Beaupré."

"I am happy to help, and they seem very much in love. It is refreshing to share in the joys of young love."

"And it certainly helps that he is a nobleman, though he lacks the wealth I would have liked to see my niece marry into."

"Wealth, he will accumulate, I am sure, but love within the bonds of marriage is rare. Charlotte will be quite happy, I have no doubt," I assured her. "Has she finished with the arrangements for the wedding?"

"Ugh," Madame d'Estrades groaned. "Not at all. The wedding details have done nothing but upset our nerves."

"Why don't you have her visit my apartments tomorrow. Come at ten in the morning. My doors won't be available to the public until eleven. I'd love to hear more about the wedding and share some of my own ideas."

The King was, again, in one of his dark moods that only I could get him out of. We escaped to the small château that he, with the help of Pâris Montmartel, purchased for me. The estate was really quite small, and served as a perfect escape for us to enjoy a private moment away from Court.

I knew that privacy was what the King required most right now, when he had so much on his mind. For years the harvest was not producing what was needed, and the citizens of Paris were in an uproar. Accusations mounted, blaming the King and me for exorbitant spending, Paris was filled with vagrants who came from the countryside to seek employment and found none, and riots were breaking out at every corner of the city. Soon enough, sinister and incredulous stories quickly spread, telling that the King snatched vagabond children from the streets and used their blood in the baths of the Prince. I tried to comfort the King, but he was deeply hurt by what his people thought of him, and it required my best efforts to lighten his mood.

Meanwhile, the tension between the Church and the government continued to mount, and the King found himself trapped between traditional values and modernity. Monsieur de Machault, Controller-General of Finance, had been pursuing the re-evaluation of the *dixième* tax, in which citizens were taxed, but the clergy and the nobility were not. Instead, he proposed for the *vintième* tax to be levied on everyone. The Church was outraged, and rejected the new tax entirely, stating that the profits belonged to God and would be used for public worship and assistance to the poor, and that the State had no right to it.

After the war, the country found itself in ever-increasing debt. The King and I agreed with Machault's idea of a tax that all must pay, including the aristocracy, who had always evaded the tax. But I also worried about how his decision to not lend the sovereign's support to the Church would personally affect the King. He was a deeply religious man, but, to the chagrin of his family and the Church, he refused to take the sacrament, confess, and take communion. He refused to behave like a hypocrite and ask for forgiveness for his infidelity to the Queen, when he was only going to continue in the same sin. Though Paris recognized that a king would naturally take a mistress, even considering it a sign of his virility, they did not accept that he would abandon his religions rights as king. This only served to further outrage the Parisian mobs against his Majesty. So the King, who wanted so badly to please the conflicting desires of the Church and his people, was depressed at finding he could please neither.

I no longer joined the King on his hunt, my health wouldn't allow it. Instead we rode the horses out to the bank overlooking the Seine.

"The Parisians, I admit, can sometimes be impossible to please," I told him. "They don't recognize the generosity and devotion of their master."

He kept silent, and stared out at the slow movement of the water. I needed a solution, a way for him to strengthen the relationship with his people. I needed to find a way for the Parisians to recognize the King's devotion to his country.

"I am told that Montesquieu's *L'Esprit des Lois* has been very well received in Geneva," I began. "Have you had the occasion to read it, Sire?"

"The clergy determined that it remain censored," he answered flatly.

"I understand, but perhaps it's time that you overrule its prohibition."

"It's hardly an appropriate time to further enflame the Church," he countered.

"The Church openly defies your wishes, despite its affects on the citizens you are sworn to protect." He looked at me, his eyes opening wide, surprised at such a reckless remark against the clergy. "We have no choice but to confront the financial losses of the war, and soon enough the harvests will improve, and those foolish rumors will disappear. What is of much greater consequence is the legacy you create."

"Once they called me *Le Bien-Aimé*, now they accuse me of the murder of their children."

"You are, and will always be the "well-loved," by all who know you," I said, taking his hand in my own and kissing it. "Your kingdom will remember you not for your own self-aggrandizement, as other kings are remembered, but for your love of philosophy and art, for your advancement of science, and for the well-being of your beloved citizens. Montesquieu, as well as the work of the *Encyclppédistes*, these are the innovators of Paris, known and respected throughout Europe. They cannot be stifled by the conservative dogma of past tradition. Instead they should be supported. Paris must see that the King of France encourages the development of philosophy and the expansion of human knowledge."

The Spring of 1751 began with misfortune. In the beginning of March, the Comtesse de Mailly, the King's former lover, died in Paris. The King had always succumbed to the morosity of death, even more so than most, and had an odd fascination with death. I assumed it was because of the death of so many of his family members at such a young age. But the loss of a woman that he had shared a portion of his life with, a woman close in age to him, startled him. And although she was at one time his mistress, I, too, felt remorse for her passing, and remembered the kindness she showed me that evening at the party when she asked me to sing.

The 25th of April, 1751, the King and I joined the wedding party at Bellevue in celebration of the marriage of Madame d'Estrades' niece, Charlotte-Rosalie de Romanet and the Comte de Choiseul. We had just finished construction on the Bellevue château less than five months ago, and it was truly a chef d'oeuvre. I worked very closely with the architect, as well as the artists and artisans, to ensure that the construction was exactly the taste à la française that I desired.

The wedding was to take place at Bellevue on the plateau that offered a panoramic view of the Seine. I looked forward to this celebration with great expectation, hoping that it would help to distract him from the misfortune and dilemmas he constantly faced.

"All the ministers will be attending," he pointed out. "I know this wedding is important to you, and I thought it would be appreciated if they came."

"You are too good to me, my love. I could not ask for a better friend."

Madame d'Estrades felt overwhelmed with the particulars of the wedding planning, and was kind enough to allow me to involve myself in many of the details. This, in itself, became a much-needed distraction for the King, who needed something to provide reprieve for him from the overwhelming concerns of the Court. The wedding of the young couple in love was a welcome diversion.

"And you've arranged for the gifts to be delivered to them before the wedding?" he asked.

"Just as you suggested, but I thought it would be very touching if you present them with their wedding gift. After all, it was your idea that they honeymoon at Crécy."

The King sat back in his chair, a gentle smile spreading across his face. It was the most relaxed I'd seen him in too long. The joy and youthful energy of a wedding of a couple in love was exactly what his spirits needed, and it put my heart at ease to see him back to his normal self. Perhaps this was exactly what he needed, the spirit and freshness of youth.

Madame d'Estrades was announced, and Madame du Hausset removed the documents the King left for me to review, and placed them on my desk for later.

"I wanted to tell you," she said, looking at my desk where the documents were just placed, "it means the world to me to have my niece so close," said Madame d'Estrades, her eyes warm with gratitude.

"The pleasure is as much mine as it is yours," I said. "She is a delightful young lady, full of spirit and vibrancy."

"She had the most wonderful time at the opera, and hasn't ceased from mentioning the great honor she felt at having sat next to you. You must know how much she admires you, Madame."

"That's kind to say," I smiled. "I am glad to know she is enjoying herself, and I look forward to her and her husband joining us at the *petite souper*. The King, as you know, greatly enjoys their company."

Since the wedding, I decided that Madame de Choiseul and her husband would be a welcome addition to our intimate circle of friends, and made a point to invite them to all of the parties. The young lady had a charming sense of humor, and was full of grace and *esprit*. The young couple's presence brought a breath of fresh air to our private gatherings, and I personally found great pleasure in acting as a mentor to her. After all, Versailles was an unforgiving world, and I had the ability to use my influence to help her and her husband. I planned to use my position to establish them in the hierarchy of Versailles.

"Yes, of course we will be there, arriving together. By the way," she said. She tried to sound casual but her voice betrayed her, rising to nearly a slight shriek as it did every time she was about to request a favor, "have you given any further thought to a position at Court for le Comte de Choiseul?"

I smiled to myself. "You are a very good aunt to concern yourself so much in the advancement of your family." Madame d'Estrades had, I admitted to myself, succumbed to the allures of Versailles. The prestige of titles and positions was too great of a temptation to resist, and I had to acknowledge that my friend had, for better or for worse, entirely become a true courtier.

"Forgive me for burdening you with this, but I can't help but worry," she said, "the young comte is such a pleasant young man, but has hardly a penny to his name. It would be shameful if we didn't do something to help him."

"You must know me well enough by now to know that I ensure that my friends are taken care of. Their positions will be announced soon enough, but there's no hurt in telling you now. Madame de Choiseul is to be given the position of lady-in-waiting to Princesse Henriette, and her husband is to be appointed as gentleman-in-waiting to the Dauphin." I could tell Madame d'Estrades was weighing the fiscal value and prestige of each role, saw the benefit of proximity to the royal family, and seemed satisfied. "There is no need for me to mention this, as Monsieur de Choiseul is, I'm sure, incredibly devoted in his work, but perhaps remind him that this position is merely a first step, and promotion is sure to follow. I will personally be sure that his efforts are rewarded, and I have an eye on a more financially advantageous position, that of inspector general of the Infantry."

"You are too generous, Madame. My family is beholden to you."

"I find enormous pleasure in helping my friends in anyway that I can."

The wife of one of my most loyal friends, the Marquis de Gontaut, requested a private reception with me. The couple was among the most respected and honorable courtiers I'd met at Versailles, and Madame de Gontaut frequently surprised me at her ability to express her thoughts in a most direct, yet eloquent manner.

"After so many years of friendship, dear Marquise, I cannot think of a single occasion in which you've required a private audience with me. I know there must be a pressing matter on your mind, and I beg you to please speak plainly."

Despite the gentleness of her nature, she sat erect in her chair and looked me firmly in the eyes. "After so many years at Versailles, I need not tell you that courtiers are not friends."

"But you and your husband are both courtiers and are of my very dear friends," I said.

"That is true, my dear. But there are always exceptions." She shifted uncomfortably in her chair. "I fear that you trust too easily, that you consider too many of these people that pay you court as friends when really, they come only to benefit themselves."

I noticed a mounting tension in the room. "Madame de Gontaut, there must be something specific on your mind. Please don't hesitate to express your thoughts to me."

"There have been rumors," she began.

"There will always be rumors," I interrupted, fearing what she might say.

"Correct, but this is of a ruse that you can ignore no longer," she stated firmly. "And, I fear that this is one intrigue you will not be able to protect yourself from."

"Are you concerned that the King has a mistress? Don't worry, Madame. They are nothing more than poor, uneducated young things that he amuses himself with. They mean nothing to him."

"This is not a mere liaison with one of the young ladies from the Parc aux Cerfs. This is a serious threat, a woman of the aristocracy. I'm speaking of the Comtesse de Choiseul."

"Madame d'Estrades niece? No, I'm sure you're mistaken," I said, putting down my tea. I was sure that such gossip was based entirely on false accusations. "I'm sure it's just a rumor that was meant to damage the happiness of a friendship. She is a very kind, sensible young woman, and loves me as if I were her aunt. She fancies herself as a sort of pupil of mine, and has been nothing but grateful for my assistance to her and her husband at Court."

"She has been behaving as a pupil? What do you mean by that?"

"Nothing of consequence, just that she seems to watch me, or imitate me."

"She imitates you?" she said, snapping her tongue. "Of course! Don't you see, she is mimicking you. Your habits, your mannerisms, it is what makes the King comfortable around you more than anyone else. The ease and familiarity that your words and behaviors bring the King is one of the foremost reasons he could never replace you. And if the Comtesse de Choiseul is able to do the same, how much easier it would be for her to take your place."

"But Madame d'Estrades would never allow it," I countered, unwilling to believe the slander against my friends. "It is because of me that Estrades is even at Court. And she has profited immensely from me. I made sure she received the position of lady-in-waiting to the King's daughter and all the wealth that position offers. And it is because of me she enjoys such nearness to the King."

"Indeed. In fact, he sits between you and Madame d'Estrades every evening, does he not? Such proximity provides her the rare ability to influence him. Besides yourself, she must be one of the few courtiers that understands the King's needs and disposition the most. How easily it would be for Madame d'Estrades to guide her young, charming niece into your place. Yes, you are right, it's because of all you've done for her that she is now one of the most powerful women at Court. And despite all you have done, she is, and has always been envious of you. Keep in mind, the Comte d'Argenson constantly whispers in her ear that you act like prime minister to the King, adding fuel to her jealousy of you. You must see how she loathes that you were once nothing but a bourgeoisie and now you reign supreme."

"Argenson will always find nasty things to say about me. I've tried making peace with him for ages, and yet he insists on remaining my enemy. Madame d'Estrades knows that, she would give little credit to whatever he has to say about me."

"It is all but acknowledged fact that the King has taken Madame de Choiseul as a lover," she stated matter-of-factly. "I would not warn you of it if there was room to doubt. And I am not the only one to suspect that Madame d'Estrades has become the mistress of Argenson. If that proves to be true, than you can expect that she will have little qualms betraying you to appease the man she adores."

And still, the King continued to visit my apartments as always, as if nothing had changed. For my part, I acted as if nothing was the matter. I showed no signs of suspicion, and behaved just as I had in the past when I felt the sting of the little romances he enjoyed at the Parc aux Cerfs. This could be nothing more than a passing fancy, I reasoned to myself, but in my heart I worried that it was serious, if this would be the end of my life as *maitresse en titre.*

Since I moved into the old rooms of Madame de Montespan, the King took up the habit of taking the private staircase to my apartments. He seemed to arrive at the most unexpected hours, and so I made a point of rarely leaving. But even within the confines of my rooms, within days, I was to discover that everyone knew about his affair with Madame de Choiseul, and she considers herself all but the declared *maîtresse* of the King.

Sitting alone in my rooms, I couldn't help but think of Madame de Montespan, the great love of Louis XIV. For years, she enchanted her lover with her droll humor, intelligence and striking beauty. But after bearing the King seven children, her beauty faded, as did his interest in her. Was I, also, to lose the interest of the King? Was I no longer capable of pleasing him, of entertaining him and distracting him from the weight of his responsibilities? And now, after all these years, was I too, to be abandoned?

By the end of September we arrived in Fontainbleu. On October 17, I was to be presented in the King's Study for the *prise de tabouret*, the taking of the stool. It was an honor given to only the highest dignitaries, in which I would be entitled to sit on a stool, as opposed to standing, while the royal family ate.

The King desired that I be honored with the title of duchess. During my presentation, he arranged for me to be followed by Madame d'Estrades and Madame de Choiseul. I could only imagine what the courtiers would whisper. "The King's young lover follows a step behind his old *maitresse en titre*. Soon enough she will take Pompadour's seat, as well as her title," they would say, satisfied with their wit. I was hurt at such insensitivity on the part of the King as to have her escort me, when she was only moments from taking my place. But I refused to resist his command. Instead, I remained silent, holding all these things in my heart.

This new title, I expected, was nothing more than a farewell gift. After all, it was his nature to strike without warning. Every minister that the King has ever dismissed has endured a similar experience. One moment they are in the company of his Majesty, and the next, quite unexpectedly, they receive a note that they are exiled to the countryside and must not visit with anyone before departure. This title, I acknowledged, was a way for him to dismiss me with dignity, a gesture of love in remembrance of our years together. There was nothing more to be done than to accept the inevitable.

The next evening, at Fontainbleu we watched the premier of Jean-Jacques Rousseau's new opera, *Le Devin du Village*. The opening lines began with,

"I have lost all my happiness,

I have lost my young lover…"

I could not have felt these lines more profoundly. I bit my lip, and focused on managing my breath to calm my breaking heart. The King sat next to me, and I took advantage of the precious little time we had left together to hold his hand throughout the performance. I did not know for how much longer I would have the honor of holding that hand I adored so much. Rousseau sat just across from us, awaiting our reaction. I smiled at him, hoping to reassure him of his success. His moment of triumph had arrived, and I feared that Madame de Choiseul's had as well.

CHAPTER XXII

"Madame, I beg you to grant a meeting to Monsieur de Stainville."

"Monsieur de Gontaut, please, insist no more on bettering my relation with your brother-in-law. I know he is a great friend of yours, but he and I have never gotten along, and now more than ever, I do not desire to see him." Years ago Monsieur de Stainville and I had met, and I found his manner unpleasing. But Gontaut promised that it was merely an oversight, and if I only gave him a chance, I was sure to find him very amusing.

"Please, Madame. I know he is a relation of Madame de Choiseul, but he says that he has urgent news for you that will put your mind at ease." I'd never seen Monsieur de Gontaut so upset. As one of my most loyal friends, he was nearly as worried as I over the threat of the King's affair.

"Then let him deliver it," I said flatly. But the more Monsieur de Gontaut begged Stainville to reveal the information, the more he resisted. He acted as if it were a game, and had no pity on my nerves and was unmoved by my tears.

Gontaut returned to my chamber. "The Comte de Stainville desires that you understand the value of his friendship for you by his willingness to share the sensitivity of this information with you."

"Of course I do. I beseech him with all of my heart, enter and tell me what he has to say."

Standing tall, the Comte de Stainville entered my room and bowed respectfully.

"Madame, forgive me," he began, handing me his handkerchief. "I did not mean to upset you. I only wish for you to understand that I am a man who desires your friendship."

I had never taken this man for a courtier. He always seemed like a soldier with little taste for the Court, but he proved to be well-adept at manipulation.

"I hope to bring you comfort in knowing that my cousin, the Comtesse de Choiseul, is to be sent away from Court," he said, softening his voice and producing a letter.

I immediately recognized the King's handwriting. As I read the contents of his letter, I felt my heart sink to my stomach.

"What is it, my dear? Your face looks ashen," said Monsieur de Gontaut.

I looked up at him. "She is pregnant. She is being removed from Court to give birth to the King's child." I closed my eyes and lowered my head. "I am to be sent away."

Rising to my feet, I turned to the Comte de Stainville. "Thank you for delivering me this news, but it has only caused me greater grief."

"All is not lost," he stated calmly. "Allow me to tell you how I attained this letter. My cousin is young, and with youth comes pride and foolishness. It is the only excuse I can think of for such boastfulness and indiscretion. This very evening, she held the letter before me like an award, and indeed it is. Madame de Choiseul had just returned from the rooms of Madame d'Estrades, who sat with le Comte d'Argenson and Doctor Quesnay."

"Doctor Quesnay was there? Has he forsaken me as well?" I cried, exasperated at what I was hearing.

"Have no fear of the loyalty of Doctor Quesnay, Madame," he said. "He had no part in this. When Madame de Choiseul announced that the King had confirmed that she was to be declared, and you were to be sent away, Argenson was quick to promise that the Doctor should have no fear in his position being affected. But the Doctor immediately removed himself from the room, and declared that, rise or fall, he would stand by your side."

I closed my eyes, exhaling deeply. Slowly it sank it, I had been deceived and abandoned by those that I loved most.

"Monsieur le Comte de Stainville, I thank you for your honesty and for bringing this to my attention. I fear there is little I can do to reward you for your loyalty to me during the moments of my disgrace. Please, do me the kindness of leaving the letter of the King with me. Monsieur de Gontaut will deliver it to you in a few days time."

Alone, I sat in my apartments, waiting for the King. I knew he would come, just as he always did, to enjoy the familiarity of my company and discuss the day's events. Finally, he arrived.

"No hand written note?" I asked, my voice as cold as ice. "I've been expecting to receive a note from you today or tomorrow, just like the ministers you've dismissed in the past, requesting my immediate departure from Court. I beg your Majesty to save yourself the trouble, I will soon remove myself."

He stood there, stunned at what I, his most faithful companion, was saying to him. Taking my key, I opened the lock to the private files on my desk and placed the envelope on the table before him. As soon as he saw it, he recognized it as his own, and immediately knew what I spoke of.

"How did you attain this?"

"Her cousin delivered it to me himself. The little traitor gloated to him of how she had succeeded in overcoming you, winning you like a prize."

I knew her behavior would upset him. There were few things he detested as much as indiscretion. He opened the letter, quickly scanning over what he himself had written to his lover, and realized his duplicity towards me.

"You've found someone to give you what I cannot – a child – and now I am to be cast aside. I have been betrayed by my closest friend, Madame d'Estrades, who has plotted against me with my great enemy, le Comte d'Argenson. Together they used this young girl to remove me from your life. She will be nothing more than a pawn, which, secured under their control, can influence you." I stood up, and paced the room. "This is the Court I've endured, regardless of what it's done to my health, just so that I could be near you. Yes, Madame d'Estrades has betrayed me, but her disloyalty is nothing compared to your own. I have stood by you, regardless of the wickedness of courtiers who demean me for nothing more than being of the bourgeoisie. For years, I've endured the hurtful insults of the Parisians who write those cruel *Poissonade* poems and pass them out in the streets, just to mock me. My sole consolation has been to bring you comfort and happiness, to help you bear the ever-increasing demands of the Crown. I have sacrificed any alternative life I could have had, because I love you."

I realized it was over. The King made his choice, he chose another. This would be the last time he saw me. Tears poured down my face thinking that I would never again be near the man I loved since I was a child. "You have been my entire existence. I've loved you with every ounce of my being, and closed my eyes to your infidelity. It was only your heart that I wanted, and now you take even that from me. To love you and share a life together, it's all I've ever wanted from you. Is my great misfortune that I've succeeded in achieving my greatest desire?"

Never before had the King seen me react this way. Never had I said a harsh or critical word to him. I stood, and paced to the fireplace. "And now a younger woman seduces you, and you so easily set me aside. No," I declared, letting him feel the full emotion of my anger, "there is no one that has used me the way you have. And no one who has been so blind as you, as to be manipulated by an eighteen-year-old flirt who fancies herself the next *maîtresse en titre*. She is no more in love with you than any other courtier whose mission is to improve their position through proximity to the Crown. Look at her indiscretion. How easily she boasts of conquering you, a spiteful success only achieved through forcing you to sacrifice your most loyal servant."

The King sank into a chair, and held his head in his hands. His eyes were closed, but I could still see tears forming along his thick, dark eyelashes. Even then, in the moment I felt most betrayed by him, I couldn't endure seeing the one person I loved most in the world cry.

I went to him, sitting before him on my knees. With my face just inches from his own, I held his beautiful head in my hands and kissed his forehead.

"Just let's spend this one last night together. Tomorrow I will go, but tonight... Let us have tonight," I said, tears running down my face.

He fell to his knees before me, placing his hands over my own.

"My dearest friend, I have been a fool. Please, please forgive me. There is no one in my life that has meant more to me that you, no one that I've trusted and depended on like you. I cannot promise that there will be no other woman to share my bed…" he said, but I couldn't wait for him to finish.

"I can't expect you to live without passion," I cried, tears swelling in my eyes. "I don't want you to be stifled from any of the joys of life, including intimacy, on account of me. I know I can't give you that, and I would never take it from you. All I ever wanted was to be your companion."

"Our friendship," he whispered, holding me tightly to his chest, his breath warm in my ear, "and my confidence in you, it can never be replaced, and will only grow more solid. I swear to you, you will always be at my side."

Shortly thereafter, Madame de Choiseul and her husband were removed from Court and sent to the countryside where she gave birth. Sadly, both the mother and her son died soon after his birth.

There was no denying it. Our relationship had forever changed. We knew it, and it was only a matter of time before the entire Court would know it as well. But I meant what I said. I could accept that I would no longer be the lover, the true *maitresse*, of the King. But it didn't change how I felt about him. I loved him entirely, and his companionship was what I wanted most. Really, it was what we both needed most.

Despite what the courtiers and Parisians assumed, my existence at Court cost me a great deal, and I was undeniably wealthier and healthier at Etioles. But it would be impossible for me to leave the King now. Each day he leaned on me more. In the privacy of my apartments, he found a refuge he could find nowhere else. My time was entirely occupied with dozens of hand-written correspondences and visits from courtiers, ministers and ambassadors. I joked with him that I deserved the same privileges of a minister, but truly I had become his own personal secretary. I realized that his trust in me had developed into a form of dependence, and even when I toyed with the idea of retiring to a more leisurely lifestyle, I couldn't bear the thought of abandoning him to the overwhelming pressures of the Crown.

"Tell me, how was your meeting with Monsieur Duverney?" I asked eagerly.

"You, ma chérie," he said, walking over and pouring me a glass of champagne, "will be very glad to learn that he has somehow managed to find the funding for your project."

For ages I had been writing to Pâris Duverney about my wishes to establish the Ecole Militaire, a school for sons of officers of the nobility. I clasped my hands over my mouth, and laughed out loud with joy. "I can't imagine how he managed it, but he somehow always finds a way."

The King walked over and placed the crystal goblet in my hand. "It's rather an ingenious scheme. Duverney will be introducing the young Italian who conceived of the idea tomorrow. His name is Giacomo Casanova."

"Casanova, I know of him," I said, smiling. "But I haven't heard of him in what feels like a lifetime. The last I remember of him was during a performance at the Opera. He gathered quite a bit of attention with a droll comment about a beautiful young actress. You will find him very clever, I'm sure."

"I am more interested in this concept of his. It's a lottery, and sounds like it could be very lucrative."

"Is there risk involved?"

"More than I'd like, but in any endeavor there will always be risk involved. And based on the estimates of Duverney, the profits greatly outweigh the jeopardy of a loss," he answered.

"If Monsieur Duverney supports the enterprise, then it will certainly be a success. I've come across few gentlemen with his insight and performance." I still remembered how the Pâris brothers rescued my family from dire financial loss by instructing us not to invest in John Law's stock market.

I leaned forward, and stroked the King's cheek with the palm of my hand. "The people of Paris will be deeply touched at the interest you show in their well-being. For so many of these young boys, you are preparing a future for them that they would have otherwise been at a loss for." At the Ecole Militaire, boys aged from eight to eighteen would gain an education and receive training that would allow them to attain a military skill set that would prepare them for a career in the army. Upon graduation, they would be provided with a commission into the army and a year's stipend.

"I can hardly take credit for this," he said, placing his hand on top of my hand that still lingered on his cheek. "This was entirely your doing, and I want you to lead it. I want you to work hand-in-hand with Monsieur Gabriel and oversee the architecture of the building."

"This, your Majesty, is your legacy, your gift to future generations. This will be an emblem of the glory of Louis XV."

FIN

BIBLIOGRAPHY

Berly, Cécile. *Lettres de Madame de Pompadour.* Paris: Perrin, 2014. Print.

Bertière, Simone. *Les Reines de France au temps des Bourbons: La Reine et la Favorite.* Paris: Fallois, 2000. Print.

Casanova, Giacomo, and Willard R. Trask. *History of My Life.* New York: Harcourt, Brace & World, 1966. Print.

Du, Hausset, Fs Barrière, St.-A Berville, Fs Barrière, and J Tastu. *Mémoires de Madame du Hausset, Femme de chambre de Madame de Pompadour: avec des notes et des* éclaircissemens *historiques.* Paris: Baudouin frères, libraires, rue de Vaugirard, no 36, 1824. Print.

Mitford, Nancy. *Madame de Pompadour.* London: Hamish Hamilton, 1954. Print.

Pevitt, Christine. *Madame De Pompadour: Mistress of France.* New York: Grove Press, 2002. Print.